Lemons Tell No Lies

Gary the Lemon Cheesecake

First edition 2025

ISBN: 9798275489330

Content Warning: Gary here. Novella contains a bitter tang of strong profanity (full, sour spectrum of it), surreal graphic violence (mostly against lemons), magic mushroom usage (psilocybin, I think they call it, wouldn't know. Stop looking at me like that! I don't!), Suggestive and tactical sexual situations, and intense psychological distress / psychosis. Reader discretion advised. Stay lemony.

"The trouble with having an open mind, of course, is that people will insist on coming along and trying to put things in it." — Terry Pratchett

"He means lemons, obviously!" — Gary the Lemon Cheesecake

Prologue

Hi there, I'm Gary, the interdimensional sentient lemon cheesecake.

You're about to follow a chap who's as paranoid as he is professional. Proper procedural investigator, this guy, but when he's best mates with a fridge called Frank, and interrogating cheesecakes, you might question his grip on objective reality. Is he brilliant or barmy? Fabulous or feckless? Strawberry or lemon?

What even is reality, anyway? I'm a sentient cheesecake, mate.

Yeah, I agree. Too bloody early in the book for that existential crisis. Well, sod off then. Go read. Or don't, I'm not your dad. Unless I am, in which case, I'm still out fetching the milk. Could be your old man, honestly—bit of a tart, me.

Stay Lemony,

Gary.

Chapter 1

"Absolutely, sir! Best savings rate on the market right now," I said, for the fourth bloody time, definitely meaning it.

"Pardon?"

Bugger. His hearing aids must be out of batteries or something. Thank fuck it's nearly home time, get back to Janet, and my darling little Jessica. Assuming Janet hasn't dropped our daughter off with the sitter and buggered off out again that is.

"Here's a leaflet, sir."

Finally remembered I can just make him read the info instead of trying to scream it at him. Thank fuck for that.

"Sorry, mate, my eyes aren't what they used to be. What were you saying?"

Bugger. Next hour is going to drag, I'm sure of that. Maybe if I pray real hard God will have mercy and smite me on the spot? Can only hope.

"Five percent! Five! FIVE! Industry leading savings rates, sir!"

"Oh sonny! You're a good looking young man, but I'm happily married."

Seriously? Seriously.

What if I press the silent alarm under the counter? Get the old bill here, save me from this doddering old git. Having to repeat myself eight bloody times should count as him holding me hostage. Could go for a bank robbery right now, get me out of this bloody conversation.

"Next please?" I announce, perhaps a little less politely than I'd intended.

"How dare you! I only have sex with my wife!"

Christ almighty. At least he's shuffling out of here now, like my rapidly decaying sanity.

"Martin, a word please?"

Here we go. My manager always had it in for me, always trying to get me to volunteer for things both in and out of the office. Wonder what I've done wrong this time? Too long in the bathroom? Tie too tight? Head still on my shoulders? Let's find out.

Followed Hannah to the private room, sat opposite her at the desk. Tie clutched at my throat a little. Seems she had a new bag, looked fancy. Branch manager, clearly on a far better wage than a peon like me.

"Customer wants to withdraw ten grand, but we have courier suspicions. You're my best guy—can you take care of it for me Marty?"

Ah. Another one of these? Seem to be on the rise lately. Made sense, the scam preyed on loneliness, and Norfolk had that in spades.

Star in your own little sting operation, only you're the mark handing over your life savings. Fucked up.

Still, Janet did love hearing my tall tales of saving customers from scammers. All this time married and I still hadn't bored her.

"Yes boss, send them in."

"Great. Customer name Hannah Stevens, I'll get her up on screen."

"Same exact name as you, boss? You related? Clone? Maybe she's here to scam you!"

Hannah chuckled a little. "No, no. Not related, just a coincidence."

"Well you know what Yoda said, there are no coincidences, only the force."

"You and your bloody Star Wars! You do make me smile, silly twit. Right, she's here, do what you do best. Don't let me down, Marty."

Probably would. Talent of mine, that.

Hannah scraped her chair across the carpet, stood to leave. Before long, replaced by an elderly woman bearing her name. Even looked a little like her, actually—maybe Hannah from the future? Wouldn't that be fun, or at least a break from this mundane courier fraud shite.

"Please, take a seat," I gently suggested.

"Where love? Car boot sale? Might get a fiver for it."

Oh her sense of humour was delightful. Disarming, too, which immediately put me on edge. Shuffled back in my seat and stared her right in the eye.

"So, ten grand was it? What's it for?"

"Oh, simple deary. It's for beeswax. As in, none of yours."

Smug smile on her face, tightening my tie with her eyes. Not so simple, this one. Zesty old dear.

"So just so you're aware, fraudsters often ask people in your position to withdraw funds from their banks, stating they're investigating counterfeiting or corruption."

She wasn't listening. Hopefully she will now.

"You would NEVER be asked by legitimate law enforcement or financial representatives to withdraw funds, and any coaching or training these fraudsters give about this speech just ensures you don't pay due diligence."

Bastards coach them, tell them we'll say that. Thinks she's onto me, star of her own little sting.

"They told you exactly what we'd say, didn't they? I've told you no lies—you'll lose every penny and we won't reimburse you a single one."

Cocky smile on her face seemed to soften significantly. Yeah, she knew. Bring it home, Marty.

"Mind placing your phone on the desk for me?"

"What!? No I'm on it—I mean, I didn't bring it."

Phone call to the fraudsters, phone in top pocket. Make sure she doesn't feel alone in here with me, whilst also probably telling her she's under caution—or some bollocks to that effect. Clever cunts.

"I'm here to help. Trust me. Show me. Phone, table."

"I... I can't. I'm under caution. Just give me the money."

Called it.

"Courier waiting nearby? Been given a codeword before you hand them the cash? They've probably called it evidence, haven't they. Reminds you of the stakes, separates you from the fact that it's actually cold, hard cash."

She shuffled in her chair, sweat beading her brow. Produced her phone, slapped it on the desk as her hand shook.

In a call with an unknown number. Bastards. I hit the red button for her, ending it. Scum.

Next half hour was spent safeguarding, referring, all that boring bollocks. I'm sure she'd have quite a tale for the police and the spouse, though for us just a Tuesday.

Thinking of which, time to go home to my family, but not before grabbing the wife a lemon cheesecake from the corner shop first, and does adore her bloody lemons. Do like to put a smile on her face too, honestly. Grab a strawberry one too, daughter and I can share that. Everyone's happy.

Pulled up out front, fumbling for my keys. Jammed them in the lock, in I went.

"Honey, I'm home!"

Could smell tomato and basil, pasta plated up on the side. My wife sure did know how to cook—when she could be bothered, anyway.

Janet appeared from the doorway, but wasn't smiling. I frowned, placing the cheesecakes on the side.

"Where's poppet?" I asked.

"She's with the sitter. Come sit in the living room Marty, we need to talk."

Oh boy. What have I done this time? Left the toilet seat up again? Socks next to the laundry basket? I'm definitely in the dog house. Buy myself a kennel.

Sat on the sofa, smiling at my gorgeous wife. But hers was visibly absent. Knot in my stomach. This felt... Different. What was going on?

"Look Marty, no easy way to say this, but I'm leaving."

"Wait. What?"

"Afraid so. I'm a lesbian."

"Wait, what? But we had sex last night?"

"Relapse."

"Wait, what?"

"Afraid so. I met a woman. I'm so sorry, Marty."

"Wait... What?"

"Yeah I know. You must be shocked. She's not gay, though, but we'll make it work. Love is love."

"Wait—what?"

"Yeah I know. I'm sure you must be shocked. I don't really love her husband, but I tolerate him for her."

"Wait, what?"

"Yeah I know. Oh, we're moving to Australia tomorrow."

"Wait! What?"

"With Jessica."

7

"Wh—what?"

"Yeah I know. Sorry Marty, lots to take in I'm sure. Well, best get packing. Toodles."

Wait.

What?

Chapter 2

Pasta. On the side, rotten, mouldy. It was a clue, I was sure, or a key. Something about it felt connected, important.

Curtains still drawn. Kept out the light, but also the eyes. Staring, bitter eyes.

Twenty missed calls, all from Hannah. She was keen. Too keen. Same name as that customer—coincidence? There are none. None.

Cheesecakes sat on the side. Strawberry, lemon. Or was it toffee? They started to sweat now, condensation on the inside of both boxes. Wouldn't be long, and the pressure would make them crack. They'll talk. Always do. I can wait.

Hadn't heard from Janet. Poppet, either, but she was far too young to understand. Tragic. Nothing about this made sense. We were saving up to buy a new house, things were going great. All that overtime at work—what was she really doing?

What—or who?

I don't envy this guy staring at me right now, that's for sure. Look at him. Stubble, gaunt, eyes bloodshot. When's the last time he even ate or slept?

"Stop staring at me."

It was no use. Every word I spoke, he anticipated with perfect precision. He was my exact mirror, trained, perfect and precise.

Knock at the door? Oh no. They've found me. I wasn't ready for this, but I had to be brave. Knew it was just a matter of time.

Had my banana ready. It wasn't a gun, but it looked like one. Convincing enough. Right. Banana pointed and ready, door open in three, two, one...

Pulled it open and pointed my gun at... Hannah?

Quickly lowered it. Misfire would be tragic. About done with tragedy.

"Marty? You look like shit. You haven't been returning my calls, or at work in some time. May I come in?"

Good question. Didn't feel safe, but she might know something, and I needed the intel. Holstered my gun in my pocket, making sure the safety was on, and stepped aside.

Wait—do bananas have safety? I think so. They are wrapped in a protective outer layer, the skin, keeping them safe from harm and divorce and Australia and spirals and when is the last time I even slept or ate and why is Hannah STARING at me and—

"Marty? You OK? You really do look horrendous. There's... Mouldy food on the side? What the hell happened here?"

Yeah, right. Like she didn't already know. She was probably in on it. They must have sent her here to gather more info on me, keep me under surveillance. Fine, I'll play along, but I'm telling her nothing.

"Wife left me. Took Jessica. Australia."

Fuck! Betrayed by my own mouth. Never would have seen it coming. Bastard.

"Oh Marty. You poor dear."

Arms around me, hugging me like a cheesecake hugs a spoon. Not very unprofessional of her, but I didn't mind. Hugged her back. Tight, warm, close.

"Let me clear this mouldy food away."

I should stop her. Evidence, and the cheesecakes were close to breaking, sweating under the pressure. It was only a matter of time. Right. Going to tell her to stop—can't very well interrogate the cheesecakes if they're in the bin.

"Thank you, Hannah. They smell."

Mutiny, was it? This mouth doesn't seem to know I'm on his side. Pathetic, really.

Time passed. Not sure how much of it. Hannah left quite some time ago. Might be an hour, maybe a week, not sure. But I had a mission, and the steaks were high, top shelf of the freezer.

I had to prepare. Couldn't fuck this up, like I did my marriage. Focus, Martin. You've trained for this.

Produced the device from my pocket, ready for action. Pressed my finger against the biometric scanner. Fingerprint recognised—we were in.

Made it past the first hurdle, but the show had only just begun. Next up, the numbers. Had to get these right—no room for failure, no chance for error.

Was it a seven, or a nine? Bugger. That last number eluded me. I had to try and focus. Ah, I had the magic number on the fridge. Almost forgot.

"Thanks, mate," I said to Frank. Think that was his name anyway. Must be something cool—he is a fridge after all.

Number in. Tap. Sequence complete. Here we go—showtime.

"Pizza Palace, order please?"

This must be the lieutenant. But I needed the head honcho, not some foot soldier.

"Where is he? I know he's there. Let me talk to him. Don't have time for the likes of you."

"Sir, we sell pizza here. Wrong number?"

Ah! Pizza, was it? Must be code for something. Let's play along, see what we can find out.

"Yes. I'd like to order one of these pizzas, please."

"Right, I gathered that when you rang a place called Pizza Palace mate. Not exactly looking for a pony now were you?"

Bugger. He was on to me. He knew about the pony. Jig was up.

"One pony, please."

"Sir, once again, we sell pizza. Now what are you having or am I hanging up here?"

Oh no. He was going to hang the hostage if I didn't get this right. Deep breath, focus.

"One pizza, please."

"Yes, we've established that. What kind?"

Kind? Could pizzas be kind? Damn. Janet would know, but her number is disconnected. Cruel fate.

"The kind one, yes."

"Sir, I—do you want a cheese pizza?"

"Oh! I do. How lovely. Can I have cheese with that, please?"

"Sure, why not. Size?"

Crucial question. Had to get this right. No room for error.

"Sweetcorn."

"Yes, we can add that. Any other toppings? And again, what size?"

Fuck! I didn't prepare for this. What goes on a pizza? Wait! I've got it!

"Cheese."

"Right, extra cheese. Size?"

OK. Crucial part. Can't fail this. No error for room.

"It's about six inches."

"Sir we only sell nine, ten or twelve."

Oh bugger.

"Sausages."

"Yes sir, we'll put sausages, sweetcorn and extra cheese on your pizza. I'll send you a ten inch then. Now what's your address?"

"Wouldn't you like to know. I'm onto you. I know it was you."

With a click the call was over. Pizza would soon arrive, although it may be delayed given that they didn't have my address.

Fuck. Right, well, better peel back the skin and eat my gun instead.

Left the banana skin on the side. Could be a clue, yellow like a lemon. But for now, I needed to talk to a lemon cheesecake, and mine was in the bin.

Time for an excursion. Only hoped I wouldn't need my gun.

Chapter 3

"Frank mate, how do I look?"

No reply. Didn't expect one, Frank being a fridge.

Made my way through the streets of March. Small town, many people. All of them staring, watching, as I walked.

Could be they knew something. Were they in on it? They set the whole thing up, I'm sure. They stared at me, concerned faces. Could be they were involved. Could be they realised I forgot my trousers. Oh. Bloody hell, Frank. Could have warned me.

Back home, pulled on some trousers this time, up over my lemon underpants. Should probably find a shirt too, but what colour? Seemed important. Maybe purple? Lemons are yellow. They complemented each other well.

Just like my wife and I did for seven years. We were a team. We—

Too late. Gone now. Australia. Lesbian. Jessica. Husband? Cheesecake?

It all meant something. The clues were all there, and they all tasted sour like lemon.

Drained the savings, too. Joys of a joint account—joint ownership, joint liability, joint operation. Lemons and Janet, working together. Bitter betrayal.

It was time to head back out. I had my trousers, I had my purple shirt, I only wished I had my shoes and my gun.

Walking the streets. Less stares this time, which I was grateful for. Streets needed tiles, not stairs.

Here it is. I was ready. Bell chimed announcing my presence—there goes any hope of maintaining the element of surprise.

There he sat, the bastard. Blonde git thought he was safe behind that glass, but I needed answers.

"Right you," I began, "What do you know? Where's my family?"

Bugger. Wasn't talking. Had to figure out how to crack him.

"Hello sir? How can we help?"

Ah, I see Gary has henchmen. Of course he does, lemony little bastard. Right, I'll have to try this the old fashioned way. Can't get him to talk from behind that glass, and don't have my gun for leverage.

"Hello William, I'd like to purchase one please."

The man behind the counter looked a little confused. Perhaps because I knew his name, which struck me as a little odd.

"Uh, it's Mark. One what mate? Pastry? Croissant? Cheesecake? Million pounds?"

Oh, you'd like to distract me with a nice little tart wouldn't you. Maybe a croissant, possibly even a chocolate one. Clever bastard.

"Need a word with this little blonde bastard here, mate," I explained. Whether he'd let me actually talk to him? Different story. No, might have been this one, actually. That made sense.

"Um... You mean this?"

Pointed to Gary. Sat there, glaring at me. He knew something, I was sure, and I'd get the truth from him one way or another. Fine. Let's do this.

"Yeah. Hand him over."

"That's a fiver, mate."

Bloody hell. Did I have my wallet? Must have done, already given it to William.

"Here. Enjoy."

"Thanks, William."

Just like that, I had him. Right. Time to get him home, get him to talk.

Sat him on the kitchen counter.

"Right then Gary, you bitter little bastard, where's my daughter?"

Silence. Nothing. Playing hardball, are we? Not having any of it.

"I can make things very uncomfortable for you. I've got a microwave, and I'm not afraid to use it."

That would heat him up. Nothing? Bloody hell. Toughest little bastard I've ever dealt with. I don't know what lemon cheesecakes are made of, but they're hard as lemons.

"Frank mate, look after this little bastard for me," I said. Frank didn't respond, but I didn't really expect him to, being a fridge. Still, it would have been nice of him to pick the lemony bugger up himself. Guess he was tired of running, just like me.

There, Gary in the fridge. Hopefully chill out a bit in there, get him to relax, start talking. Good old Frank. Stoic, strong, reliable. Couldn't have asked for a better companion.

Other than my new gun, of course. Keeps me safe. Didn't even need ammo.

Sighed, staring at Frank. Hadn't said a word since Janet left with Jess. Hadn't before, but that was besides the point.

Think it was about time I went back to work. I can't just stay here forever. I knew they were out to get me, though, so I had to think. What if I hid in plain sight?

Show up to work, possibly with trousers? Maybe even a balaclava?

Yeah. Why not? But I needed to call Hannah first, and ask her what her favourite flower was.

Right. I'm ready for work now, I'm certain of it. Been long enough. I'll call, ask to come back in. I can do it. I'm ready.

Phone out, number tapped. Showtime.

"Pizza Palace?"

"Yes, can you connect me to Hannah, please?"

"Sir, this is a pizza place. You have the wrong number."

"How dare you! I've never been wrong about a number in my life, other than the number of years I'd spend married."

He clicked the call into oblivion, gone in a flash, just like my family, my hope, my dreams, my savings.

Right, time to call Hannah. Dialled her number.

"Pizza Palace?"

"Yes, I'd like to order one Hannah please."

"You again? Sod off, mate. Get help."

Clicked the call away again. Maybe I should get some help. Hannah was helpful—I'll try calling her.

"Pizza Palace?"

"Hannah? Is that you?"

She hung up on me. Bugger.

Oh. Lucky for me, she called me back.

"Marty, just checking in on you. Are you OK? You worried me."

How'd she have my number, anyway? This seemed a little unprofessional. Right, back to my script. Ready for work, schedule me in, good to go.

"Let's go on a date."

Hold on. What was that? That... Wasn't right. Did I just—

"Really!? Yeah, you know what? Why not? I'll fill out the paperwork. What did you have in mind? I'm so excited!"

Bugger. I genuinely had no idea, but probably something completely ridiculous. Might even be lemons.

"Restaurant in Downham Market, table booked for eight sharp."

Gibberish.

"Confidence! See you there then, handsome."

Right, well, that apparently happened. Frank silently judged me from across the kitchen counter.

"Relax Frank. It'll be fine. See what she knows. Keep chilling that cheesecake—he's bound to break soon, tart little twat."

No reply. Typical. Did like his humming, though, my Frank.

Seems I needed to get ready. But first, time for some advice from an old friend.

Chapter 4

"William, need your help mate. I've got a secret mission tonight."

"Yeah, I heard. Run it past me one more time—what exactly is your plan here?"

Could I trust him? I guess I had to. He was staring right at me, and I just didn't feel I had any other choice.

"I'm going undercover. Pretty tired, need the sleep. But before that, I'm going to a restaurant with Hannah."

"Wait, what? Why Hannah?"

Silly Willy. Didn't he realise? He could be slow sometimes. The lemons were everywhere.

"Her hair. Dyed it blonde. The same colour as LEMONS! BITTER FUCKING LEMONS!"

That should get his attention. Perhaps not, just kept staring at me instead.

"William?"

"I don't like this, Marty. You're obsessed with lemons, and you can't articulate why."

Articulate? What did that even mean? Felt like I knew, but I just couldn't articulate it.

"Well, I saw something. I know I did. I haven't quite been myself lately, I'll admit that. But I know I'm not crazy. The lemons are watching, William."

"Just be careful, Marty. Don't crack."

"Should say the same thing to you. Right. Guess I have a mission, then."

"Stay sharp, Marty."

Carefully prepared my clothes for the evening. Had to look the part. I finally decided to settle on one of Janet's dresses, left in her wardrobe. What better way to hide in plain sight.

Sadly, it didn't fit. She always was skinny. Guess I'll just wear my purple shirt again. Maybe some trousers?

Think I need to focus here. My daughter is gone. My wife is gone. Australia might as well be on the other side of the world.

"Marty? You there mate?"

"Yeah. Right, thanks for your help William. How about I meet you at the coffee shop tomorrow?"

"Sounds good mate. See you later. I'll be off."

That sorted, time to check on my boy Frank.

"Hi mate. Still chilling our guest then?"

Ever stoic, ever silent, still humming away happily. His smile was infectious. No, wait, that was just a fridge magnet.

Cheesecake would break soon, then I'd finally get some answers. Lemons tell no lies.

Got myself ready, out the door. Drive to Downham Market was filled with anticipation. I did anticipate that, though, so made sure to bring my gun. Protection.

Pulled into the restaurant car park. Nice and quiet for a... What night even was it anyway?

Still, the quiet helped. Pushed open the door, exaggerated smile from the hostess.

"Hello there sir! Did you book a table?"

"Yeah. I called my boss and asked her here."

"OK, under what name please?"

"My own, obviously."

She wasn't very bright, clearly.

"Um, and what name is that sir?"

What a strange question to ask. Didn't she know? With everyone staring, someone must have. I'll give her an alias. Safer that way.

"Fletcher. Martin Fletcher."

There. That sounded almost real.

"Great! Um, no reservations under that name?"

Bugger. I did ask Frank to call but he must have forgotten. Bloody fridge.

"Well, bugger me then. You got a table for three?"

"Yes sir, over by the corner. I'll show you."

Didn't need showing, could already see it. This one definitely skipped a few days of school.

Hold on—why did I book a table for three? Is William joining us? Or something else I've clearly forgotten? Gary?

Sat at the table, chest tight, breath heavy. The droning, the lights, the stares. Irritating. Infuriating.

Bugger, left my gun in the car. Not very smart. What if I got hungry?

"There you are, Marty," Hannah said, pulling up a chair.

She wore a red dress, covering her body like clothes. Beautiful. Clever to wear a low cut one too—very tactical, easy access to any gadgets she may have stored in her bra. Intelligent woman, Hannah. Perhaps a little too much so.

"Excellent to see you," I began. "I've ordered us some appetisers. They'll be here a minute ago."

Gestured towards the platter, glistening olives, various cheeses, all that other restaurant bollocks. When the bloody hell had I done that?

"Ah, always loved your sense of humour! So... Must confess, I figure one woman's loss is another woman's gain. Marty, I'm nearly forty, and you know, you're you."

Strange. I always was me, wasn't I? That was code, clearly. Wish Frank was here. His humming sounded a little like morse code if I focused hard enough.

Couldn't help but notice her hair. Dyed blonde. Lemon blonde. Beautiful, bitter lemon.

Shit. She was working with Gary, was she? Maybe. Right, I need to stay calm, stay focused. Mission.

"So...what do you think, Martin? Intrigued?"

Bugger, she's been talking, and I missed it. I couldn't admit that, especially without my gun for backup. Still wish Frank was here, he was big and intimidating—I'm just a scrawny git.

"Sorry, Hannah. Missed some of that. Loud in here, isn't it?"

She smiled gently and held my hand.

"Relax, just have a good time. Be with me."

Next two hours were spent enjoying food together. I ordered lemon chicken with lemon meringue for dessert. Lemonade to drink, naturally. Not shaken, nor stirred.

"Had fun tonight Martin. Think about what I've said?"

"Will do. Night."

If only I had the faintest clue what that even was. Bugger.

Chapter 5

"I mean, you could just call her Marty. Ask her to repeat herself."

Sound advice from William, but there's no way I'd let myself do that. Far too bloody proud.

"Hi Marty!" Hannah said, answering my call. Apparently. Didn't offer me any pizza this time, though.

"Uh hi, I just called to double check some stuff from yesterday that's all."

"Oh? Want me to text you the details?"

That made more sense. I could read texts, but I couldn't read words—especially spoken ones.

"No, thanks. I'll meet you at the coffee shop tomorrow."

"Right, have a good day. Are you coming back to work yet, then?"

Probably a good idea. Was getting sick of my house, Frank the fridge my only company, or sometimes William when he could be bothered. Busy guy.

Thinking of Frank, needed to check on that bitter bugger of a cheesecake. Must be chilled enough to talk by now. Time for a little chat, methinks, Gary.

"Martin?"

"Oh sorry, off with the cheesecakes. Right, yes, I'll do that. That last bit you said, which I definitely did hear."

"Great. Wear something slutty," she giggled, ending the call with a click.

What the heck did that mean?

"Frank, mate? Any ideas?"

Nothing. Bloody fridge. Fine, I'll just see about that cheesecake instead. Popped Frank open and took Gary out, carefully removing his box. He was cool to the touch. Very cool.

"Right then, you sour little bastard. What do you know? Why are the lemons following me? Where's my family?"

Nothing. All that time in the fridge, still wasn't any closer to talking. Heck of a lot cooler, though.

"I didn't want to have to do this. But I've got a knife. Please, just talk. Just give me my daughter back. I'm begging you, Gary."

Nope, cheesecake was still silent. But a thought occurred—had I bought the right one? Could this one be orange? They looked similar to lemons, right?

Put him back in his box, back in Frank. Sighed, slumped at the table. Grabbed a gun from the bowl, peeled back the skin and bit into it. Soft, sugary, delicious. Would go great sliced on top of a lemon cheesecake.

Pulled out my phone, unlocked it. Stared at the screen. Needed to talk to William—he always had a thought.

"You there mate?"

"Yeah, I'm here. What are you going to do?"

"Hannah knows something about the disappearance of my family. She knows about the lemons, too. I'm being watched. I see them follow me. She knows. They know."

"Lemons are just lemons, Marty. But keep an eye on Hannah. You told me about that expensive bag—where had that come from?"

Now that was a very sharp question. Even on a bank manager's wages, that seemed a little flash. Was she selling lemons on the side? Maybe the cheesecakes were connected. I needed to find out.

Text buzzed in—Hannah.

"Be round at eight. See you soon x"

Interesting. She could see me? I searched high and low, opened drawers, closed curtains. I found no evidence of surveillance, but Hannah was no liar. Lemons didn't tend to do that—they much preferred the bitter tang of truth.

"Frank, I need your help. I think I've agreed to a date, but I'm still not over my wife. Can you call and cancel, please?"

Nothing. Fine, Frank, maybe you're right, maybe I should do this. But before Hannah came here, I needed a plan to protect myself.

Lemons were still everywhere. Lemon wallpaper, lemon pattern curtains, Frank storing bottles of lemonade and the little citrus bastards themselves in bags by the dozen.

Even those lemon boxers Janet bought me for my last birthday. She was so proud of them. Loved lemons, as much as she loved me.

Probably more, actually, come to think of it. What with the... What happened. What she did. Who she took. Where she went.

What did actually happen? Whole night was a blur, and none of it made sense. The whole speech left a bitter taste in my mouth and heart.

Lesbian, husband, lemons, Australia—

Nope. Going to lose the lemon-scented plot if I keep going down that route. Refuse to let myself get bitter. Somewhere out there, my daughter was waiting for me to find her. I had to stay sharp.

Increments of time passed in their standard units. Minutes felt like minutes until eight in the evening, and there was a knock on my door.

It could only be one person.

"Hi William," I cheerfully stated, opening the door to Hannah.

"Marty? Who's William?"

"Oh sorry. William on the brain. My mate. Welcome, Hannah. What's that you got there?"

She had a bottle with her. Looked like... No. Can't be. Lemonade. Bottle of fucking lemonade. I knew it.

"Whenever I came before, I noticed how much of this stuff you had! Assumed you loved it, no?"

She WAS in on it. The whole thing. The lemons, the lemonade, the conspiracy—it all connected. She was here to watch me, observe me like a person seeing things.

Hold on—here before? Had she said that? Was she onto me?

"Oh, Janet was the real lemonhead. I don't mind it, though. Thanks."

Hannah smiled as she stepped inside. Same red dress from the restaurant, though noticeably her lemons were positioned in a more tactical manner, raised, squished.

"Oh hey! You've got a lemon cheesecake here. Want to eat it?"

She made herself right at home. Opened up Frank like a fridge, didn't even buy the guy dinner first. Sickening.

Of course she wanted to eat the evidence. Why else would she be here, dressed in tactical gear, beautiful to behold. I needed to get her away from Frank, needed a plan.

"It's peach, actually," I incorrected. "Not going to crack."

"Crack? You mean cut? Don't worry, says lemon right here on the box. Do they even make peach cheesecakes?"

That... Was a good question. No, I don't think the council of cheesecakes approved a peach flavour. They were usually known to be quite bitter, unless they were sweet.

"No problem. That one has chilled enough, let's just eat him."

Oops. I'd have to go buy another one of the blonde buggers, but at least my apparent date was apparently happy. Bye Gary.

Cracked open the lemonade, shared a glass each. Bitter citrus burned my throat, accusing me of failure all the way down.

It hadn't lied. They left me. Lesbian, husband, Australia.

Jessica.

Time passed, more standard increments. Hannah suggested she remove her tactical gear, which seemed like a good idea. She looked far better out of it.

The next two hours was something of a blur, but I was sweating like a cheesecake under Frank's watchful gaze. Hannah left me with a smile on her face stretching to her eyes.

Something felt different now. But I was now more convinced than ever—I was going to find my daughter, and bring her home. The lemons demanded it. The lemons forbade it. The lemons deserved it.

I don't know why Janet chose to leave me. How much of her story was even true? It still made no sense—why did she need to go to Australia for lemons when they sell them right hehe? But she left regardless, and I had to know why. But more importantly—I needed my daughter back, and soon.

Chapter 6

Back at the bank now. Bought myself a yellow suit from the charity shop. Felt like it glowed, called out to me even. Blend right in with the bitter tide.

Also bought some lemon soaps, lemon shampoo, lemon deodorant. The more I surrounded myself with them, the closer I got to the truth, the less they noticed me.

Was about time I washed off the stench of my failure anyway, replace it with the bitter tang of lemon.

If only I could replace my current customer with a lemon, too.

"I don't understand," Shanice said. "I just deposited a twenty! So how the hell is my balance only two quid?"

Some people spent more time smoking weed behind the bike sheds than they did in maths lessons, it seemed.

"Your music subscription came out, and you had a pending transaction from the bakery earlier ma'am," I parroted for the umpteenth fucking time. Lemons in her ears, clearly.

"Yeah, but I put twenty in. So how's it now only two?"

Ethernet cable in the back of my computer looked pretty thick. Think it might tie into a pretty solid noose in a pinch. Less of a joke by the moment.

"May I suggest a remedial maths class?" I spoke aloud, horrified. Oh fuck. Inside voice, sour twit.

"A remedy what? What's that? Where's my money then?"

Oh thank fuck. Far too thick to even know what I'd just apparently said. Bastard mouth betraying me, running off on its own like my wife ran off with my daughter and our savings and my lemonade.

"So. Twenty minus ten minus eight equals two."

"Yeah but why is it when I put in twenty quid I only got two showing now? Are you robbing me here?"

No, but she robbed taxpayer money on school fees, clearly, just like she's robbing me of precious seconds of my fleeting existence.

"Look. You deposited the money, yes, but you already owed it. You've got an overdraft."

"A what? Is that where you give me free money?"

I swear they need to institute some kind of competency test for owning a bank account. If you need a licence to hit the road you should need one to hit my quickly eroding sanity—what remains of it, anyway.

"When life gives you lemons, eat them," I said with finality. That should settle things in a calm and respectful manner, not a cheesecake harmed.

She glared at me, opened her mouth as if to say something else. Instead she just trotted off. Good, won't need to use my ethernet noose after all. I had grown rather accustomed to breathing.

Oh. The savings man with the excellent hearing was back. Yeah, I still might need it after all. Not repeating myself two hundred and four times again.

"Martin, a word?"

Saved by the Hannah. Yellow dress complimenting her lemon blonde hair and glowing yellow eyes. Now what had I done wrong, I wonder?

Took me into her office, sat across from me at her desk. Smiled, but it didn't reach her eyes this time.

"Ahem... So last night was, well, fun. Plenty of it, in fact. But we should stay professional, and well, just be mindful. Do you understand?"

Not a word, no.

"Every word, yes."

Grinned at me, gestured to her door. Well, that was a quick chat, wasn't it. Probably had more citrus themed schemes to plan.

Couldn't trust her. Couldn't trust anyone. Someone knew something, I was sure. Maybe that girl with the twenty? She sure did ask a lot of questions. Nobody could be that bad at maths—she was gathering intelligence, observing, watching, waiting.

I was so blind. How could I not see it? I had to stay sharp. The bitter tang of failure lingered on my tongue again. It was starting to go stale.

"Hi there, I'd like to withdraw two hundred pounds please," my next customer said.

Absolutely captivating. She had fiery red hair like a redhead, and emerald green eyes like emeralds. I could tell life never gave her lemons. Well, no more than two, anyway.

"Yes, of course. Do you like lemons?" I cautiously asked.

She raised an eyebrow. "Not bad, I guess? Depends on the context. If you mean that dashing yellow suit you're wearing, then I like them a lot."

Her grin was wide, tactical. I could tell this was a sharp young woman. She must have been about my age, or possibly not.

"Name and ID, please," I stated carefully.

"Juliet Smith. Here's my passport."

Juliet? That was incredibly close to Janet. Something was wrong here. The walls started to surround me, as if I were in a building of some description. The pulsing from the lemon adverts grew brighter. Freshest savings rates in town.

Took a deep breath, and counted her money. All four hundred pounds.

"Here you go," I said, handing her the cash and her passport back. Threw in my wallet for good measure.

"Oh, oops. You gave me too much. Unless you're trying to give me a tip?" Juliet chuckled, handing me back half the money and my wallet.

Hmm... A tip? I wasn't sure if I could accept that. Kind gesture, though. What a thoughtful woman. Not just a stunning one.

I'd best just put the cash in the drawer instead. Tip the branch. Sure it would be grateful.

"Thoughtful of you," I began. "I hope you have a lovely day."

She grinned wide, pocketing the cash, before walking towards the exit. Something about the interaction seemed strange to me, though. Lemon related? Possibly.

Could it be the leather jacket, actually? Seemed unconventional with the red hair, but I wasn't exactly a master of tactical planning. More of a bank teller than anything, really.

Maybe it was the business card she slipped me? Right here, in my wallet. That could mean something. Probably not, though, so I just shoved it in my pocket. I'll give it to Frank, he likes these things—he's plastered in them.

"Well, she seemed very friendly, didn't she Martin?" Hannah said, hovering over my shoulder, apparently.

"Very tactical," I responded. "Fetching young woman. Lovely lemons."

Hannah narrowed her gaze, grin faltering. "Bit odd, if you ask me. Never seen her in here before, randomly withdraws two hundred instead of just using the ATM? What's her angle?"

Now that was one very acute question. Or obtuse? Couldn't be sure.

Chapter 7

I sat across from William in the coffee shop, waiting patiently for my latte. I'd been waiting over half an hour, and was getting frustrated.

To be fair to the staff, I may not have ordered it. But something told me if I waited patiently, it would arrive.

Held out my phone, looking to William for approval.

"I'm back to work, William. Every time a Janet walks in I'm closer and closer to wearing that cable."

"Come on now, mate," William started gently. "You'll find your daughter again. I hope."

I truly hoped I would, but lemons tell no lies. Bitter little bastards pointed and laughed at me every time I opened Frank for milk. Found myself missing his humming, sat in this boring coffee shop.

"What if I don't, William? What happens then?"

"You can't think like that, mate. How big can Australia even be? You'll find her soon enough. I'm sure of it. Keep the faith, mate."

"Sir, will you be ordering a drink?" Kind young waitress said, hovering nearby, grin wobbling.

"I'm still waiting for my latte."

"Oh! Sorry to hear, when did you order it?"

"Oh, I didn't. I'm just waiting for it."

She narrowed her gaze, grin gone. That seemed to give her pause. Was she onto me? Something about her expression felt measured, practised, as if she was used to taking and following orders from someone.

"Um, well, you want me to make you a latte then?"

"Yes, a lotte," I responded, giggling at my little pun.

Didn't make her laugh, though. She just smiled awkwardly and backed away. Didn't offer William a drink either, but he was on the phone anyway, so wouldn't do him any good.

"William?"

"Yes, mate?"

"I...I miss my family."

He just smiled, though it masked the pity and the pain. The bitter tang of loneliness dug into my ribs extra hard whilst sat here in this stupid coffee shop, drone of other patrons chatting and sipping and smiling. Buggers.

Placed my palms flat on the table, phone laid out between them. Couldn't help but feel like someone was watching me, following me. It could be that waitress, acting suspicious, scared even. Possibly the man behind the counter, whispering to her. Could be that redhead Juliet lady from the bank, who was sitting on the other side of the coffee shop, holding a newspaper.

She was staring right through me, like I wasn't there. Was it William she was interested in? Hold on—what exactly WAS she doing here?

It couldn't be a coincidence. What are the chances that someone who visits the bank in town also visits the coffee shop in this same town? They had to be small, right?

"William, am I being followed?"

"What makes you say that mate?"

"Juliet is over there in the corner. She's staring right at us. Should we go talk to her?"

No need, it seemed. She smiled, approached my table and sat across from me.

"Well hello there charming man with the yellow suit, what are you doing here? Who's your friend then?"

Juliet gestured towards my phone, smile on her face. Those piercing green eyes pierced mine like emeralds pierced lemons.

"William."

"I see. So... What brings you to this coffee shop, exactly?"

Interesting. Was this an interview? An interrogation? An exam, perhaps? I hadn't studied.

"Lemons."

That seemed like the most logical, simple answer I could give. Though in retrospect, maybe I should have said coffee. Is lemon coffee a thing? If I wait long enough, they'll bring me one.

"Oh, you tried that new lemon latte, have you? Very good. I come here to relax between my work tasks, it can get quite busy. So tell me more about you then? Let's start with your name?"

Hadn't I told her that? I was... I was sure I had. Hadn't I?

Didn't matter. I could repeat myself.

"Lemons."

Shook my head, took a breath. Not that one.

"Fletcher. Marty Fletcher."

"Oh, what a lovely name. Are you married then Marty? Good looking chap like you, must be, surely?"

My smile reached my knees. My heart my ears. My throat, dry as a lemon in the desert, baked to a husk in the blazing sun.

"Yes. I am. I was."

Her smile seemed as warm as it did judgemental. Her hand, soft, smooth like the gentle rind of a lemon atop mine.

"I see. She left, I take it?"

Couldn't help but feel like she was asking me questions, here. But why? Did I have answers or questions of my own?

"Yep. Lesbian. Husband. Australia. Jessica."

Those didn't seem like questions, more like a list. Each word a jab to the ribs, until the final jaw-smashing Jessica. Clenched my fists and glared at the table, waiting patiently for the latte I never ordered. But it was coming. I knew it was.

"You poor thing, you've been through so much, haven't you? You've got my business card. Drop me a call sometime, won't you? Let's spend some time together. I'll think of a way to cheer you up."

Her chair scraped as she pushed it back and stood to leave. I couldn't help but wonder what William would think of all this, but I hadn't the stomach to ask him. He'd only offer me some practical, thoughtful, caring advice that I was in no mood to hear.

"Sir? Will you be ordering?"

Déjà vu as a waitress approached my table again. Could swear I'd had this conversation before. Still, I'd had enough of waiting. Stood, shook my head, left.

Bitter chill of the morning air hit me like the sour tang of lemon. There she was again, Juliet, that fiery red hair. She was walking away from me, as if she'd just left the coffee shop moments prior.

She was part of this, it seemed. I needed to know why she was following me, so I kept pace, at a distance, seeing what I could find.

She walked on through the busy streets, until finally, she reached a bus stop. She stepped aboard just before it pulled away.

The bus had a banner on the side. Something about the freshest savings rates in town, with a picture of a lemon, glaring right at me.

She was definitely involved. Lemons tell no lies.

Chapter 8

Found myself sat on a bus, but my destination was unclear. It was crowded, full of people, much like a method of publicly accessible transport.

I hopped off at the next station, and waited. They were following me, I was sure, and within a few minutes I would be certain.

Made my way to the corner shop, opposite the bus stop. It was suspicious, being wedged between two other shops. No corner at all.

Bought myself another gun. Two, in fact—I was hungry. Peeled back the skin and ate it, though the soft, sweet sugary sensation quickly turned sour in my mouth, picturing my little girl smiling up at me as I read her a bedtime story.

It was cold out. The bitter winds stole tears from my eyes. But not for long—I finally found what I was looking for.

Another bus pulled up at the stop. I finally had the proof I needed—they were, in fact, following me. I needed to get some answers, and who better to ask than the man driving them?

I stepped aboard and pulled my gun on him. Pointed it right at him as he chuckled.

"Drive," I demanded.

"You're a riot, mate! I mean yeah, I was planning to, bus driver and all. You gonna eat that?"

Ah. Seemed he was hungry. Relatable.

But I couldn't surrender my gun. I needed the protection—without it, I was exposed.

"Here, you can have it."

"Thanks!"

He took my gun, peeled back the skin and ate it. Once more betrayed by the bitter zest of my bastard mouth. Seems I was unprotected now, I'd have to rely on my intuition to keep me safe.

Driver thanked me for the gun—kind of him. Time soon passed, minutes passing me by as more of them came, relentless in their zesty pace.

Changed from bus to bus a few more times. They made it easy to identify the conspirators, as the buses involved had bright, lemon themed adverts for 'fresh savings rates' on the side.

The irony was palpable. If only they knew those savings rates were actually half a percent behind the market leading institution. Cruel, bitter fate.

I followed the route for some time. It almost seemed circular, as if the buses always eventually visited the same destinations.

I recognised my location, stepping off the bus once more. It was quiet here, though, hardly a soul in sight. The High Street of Wisbech had been stagnating for quite some time. Why bother visiting a shop when you can order everything you need cheaper from online, direct to your door, I suppose.

Found myself sat next to an interesting looking young gentleman with a large puffer jacket. He was involved, too, jacket as yellow as the ripest of lemons. Swallowed hard, preparing to interrogate him, without my trusty gun.

"Hi mate, lovely weather, isn't it?" I said, mean and menacing, sharp and tangy. That should get him talking.

"Yeah bruv, nice and cool innit. So...you into herbs then mate?"

Interesting question. It seemed this guy was some kind of chef, possibly a professional based on the yellow puffer jacket adorning his body like clothes.

"I like sour ones, bitter ones. I think. I enjoy oregano, too, and lemon basil."

A real chef would instantly know those herbs. Let's see if his cover holds.

"Oh yeah, I got some very special oregano for sale here bruv, you feel me? So you interested?"

Couldn't honestly say that I was. I hadn't the ingredients to make mushroom lemon risotto, certainly not on me.

"Nah, I don't have any mushrooms. Can't use it."

The chef grinned wide, smiling up at me. There was a sharpness to his eyes, tightening my chest.

"Ahh, so that's what you're into, is it? You're not police, right?"

"No sir. Don't even have a gun."

He chuckled. "Right, right. Well I got some shrooms for you bruv, get these bad boys home and go on a trip. You feel me?"

Got my wallet out, paid the man. I was unsure what had just happened, though—I needed to go on a trip on multiple buses to get home, not the other way around.

He handed me my mushrooms in brown, tactical packaging, obscuring them from any sour gazes from passers-by. Sharp thinking—they were expensive, valuable, quality ingredients directly from a celebrity chef.

"Well, see you around bruv. Have fun."

Should pop these home to Frank, have him guard them for me. That was at least dinner sorted, but not tonight—found myself tangy for a pizza. Time to follow the buses home, avoiding the compromised lemon banners as I do, my mission a complete success.

Chapter 9

Took me a long time to get home, probably. Frank guarded my mushrooms along with the little lemony bastard. Still wasn't talking. Didn't even seem scared.

Though I did recall eating him with Hannah, some time ago? I must have captured another. Both called Gary. All called Gary.

"How's our little guest then Frank? Chilling out? Keeping cool? Cold as ice?"

I double checked Gary's cardboard prison. Could see him through the top of it, boxed up like an animal. Definitely a lemon Gary this time. Good. He'll chill in Frank until I get my answers. I grew tired of lemons and their lack of lies.

"Got you a present, Frank. Here you go mate. Know how much you like these things."

Gave Frank the business card from that red haired redhead woman, Janet.

No, Juliet. Janet is...was... My wife.

Jessica is my daughter. Was my daughter. Was my world. Was my reason for getting up in the morning. Was my reason to draw breath.

Looked over at Frank. Swear I saw him smile at me, just for a moment. My stoic friend, my constant companion, my shield against the sour citrus tide stealing tears from my bitter eyes just like they stole my family, my future.

Couldn't help but notice I was calling Juliet. The hell was I up to now? This could only end terribly, but seemed I didn't care.

"Juliet Smith, private investigation services?"

The truth shocked me like the bitter tang of lemon rind in my coffee. She was an investigator. Seemed I'd finally found myself an ally against the sour tide.

Oh. Other than Frank and William, of course. Really should get my phone out and see how he's doing.

Oh wait. I'm holding my phone. Nitwit.

"Hello?"

"Janet? Is that you?"

"No, sorry, Juliet. Who's calling, please?"

Had to think fast. Needed to give her a name, and it had to sound convincing. Frank Citrus? No, no. Larry Lemon? Bugger! I was running out of time. I needed a name, and I needed it now.

Scanned Frank, business cards all over him, worn like service medals from his time in the trenches. There had to be a name on here, one I could use, one that sounded real.

"Hello? Sir?"

Bingo. Found one.

"Martin Fletcher, teller in the lemon suit."

Perfect. That name sounded incredibly real, because it was mine. Crisis averted, cover maintained.

"Oh, lovely, the handsome chap in the yellow suit. Can we meet? Could do with a little talk, if you're up for it? My place or yours?"

That seemed unwise. Her house was an unknown quantity, a sanctuary of her own, possibly riddled with all manner of traps. I'd run out of guns again, too, so I wouldn't feel safe. Ah—I had the perfect idea.

"I'll meet you in the middle of the road outside my house. Nobody would expect us to meet there."

I had a point. It made zero sense, the roads belonged to the cars, though from time to time the motorbikes would have their say, roaring angrily as they sped on by. Nobody would expect us to stand in the road and talk.

"You've got a really quirky sense of humour! I'm coming to yours. Prepare yourself."

With a click, the call was ended. Fuck. My smile turned sour, my sanctuary soon to be invaded by Juliet. Her name so similar, yet her appearance so different. Beautiful, but nowhere near as much as my Janet. Nobody was.

Lesbian. Husband. Australia. Jessica.

Lemons.

Not my Janet anymore, though, was she. She vanished in a flash, a whirlwind, a series of words each delivering a dagger to my ribs. None so cruel as taking my daughter away. Didn't even get to say goodbye, at the sitter's when she dropped the floor out from under my world.

Lot to answer for, when I find her and get my daughter back.

If.

Juliet would be on her way. I had questions, nagging at my brain like the bitter tang of lemons in my eyes. How the hell did she know where I lived? I never told her. I never told anyone.

She was following me, it seemed. The thought turned sour, the implications heavy. Something would change today. There was an energy in the air, fit to burst, zest overwhelming.

Shook my head, trying to focus. Surrounded by them still. The paintings on the walls, lemons. The wallpaper, lemons. The curtains, lemons.

Lemons, lemons, lemons.

Everywhere.

Pulse quickened, pounded in my ears. What had I seen? Why did it matter?

Why were the bitter lemon bastards hunting me, stalking me, desperate to kick me whilst I'm down?

Collapsed onto the sofa, heart beating out of my zest. Deep breaths, eyes closed, focus.

No guns, Juliet coming. Unknown distance to my base of operations. Questions persisted that needed answering—how exactly did she know my location? Why was her hair red? If lemons are sour, why does lemon cheesecake taste so sweet? Gary would know, but the bitter little bastard just wouldn't talk. Frank would crack him, though, sooner or later. If I could count on one person in my life, it was him. Dependable as the sunrise.

Knocks rapped on the door. No gun, just my wits and Frank as backup. Felt safer with him watching over me, big and intimidating, stoic and strong.

"Watch my back, Frank. Stay frosty."

Knocks on my door again, rang sour in my ears. Deep breath, hand on handle. Time to find out what she knew, other than my address and somewhat complicated marital status.

Really wish I had my gun.

Chapter 10

"Ah. I've been expecting you," I stated to the postman standing before me.

"Should imagine so sir, I deliver your mail!"

It was true. He did, and he had a letter for me now. I half-heartedly pawed at it, eyes drawn to something else rather captivating.

On the passenger seat of his van, a lunchbox sat. Sandwiches, chocolate bar, and a gun, yellow and ripe, ready for action.

I could use that for when Janet arrived. Unfortunately, she was already here and staring at me, waiting for my business to conclude with the postman. Similarly, her name was Juliet, which also rang sour. Keep mixing those two up. Scratched at my chest a little, staring at the postman.

"Sir?"

"Oh. Right. Thanks for the gun, have a good day."

Took the letter, placed it on the side. Juliet smiled and stepped past me, the postman soon driving away with the only gun in reach. I'd have to stay sharp lest things turn bitter.

"Lovely home you got here yellow man," Juliet said, hands in her jacket pockets. She wore a black leather jacket atop her shoulders, and an incredibly tactical v-neck shirt, lemons practically on display.

Wouldn't allow myself to be distracted, though. Still had to find out what was happening, whether she was friend or foe.

"Marty?"

"Oh! Yes. Let me take your shirt. Jacket, I mean."

She shrugged and placed her jacket on my coat rack, giggling.

"Gentleman, aren't you. Right then. Let's get down to business."

Bugger. Not sure how we were supposed to do that when I had no protection. Postman had already driven off with the only gun in sight, and I didn't run a business. Just a bank teller.

Could hear Frank happily humming away as Juliet led me to my sofa, sat me down. Her smile wobbled, hint of zest behind her eyes.

"You seem a little shook up, Martin. What's been going on?"

Tactical question. Saw no harm in telling her the truth.

"Frank's holding Gary hostage. Gary isn't talking, but he knows something about the disappearance of my family."

She raised an eyebrow, her pen scratching against the paper of her little black journal. Hadn't seen her bring that in. Suppose it helped with her job as an impersonator.

"So... Who's Frank, then? And this Gary?"

Shouldn't she have known that? She was the investigator. Though, perhaps she was just being private. She could just go ask Frank herself, though he wouldn't reply. Just a fridge.

"Frank is in the kitchen. He's trying to get the little blonde bastard to chill out, but he still won't talk."

She got up for a moment, wandered to the kitchen. She was only there for a brief moment before returning, sighing as she sat closer to me on the sofa.

Her emerald eyes pierced me like the bitter tang of lemon. Her gaze narrowed, her notebook placed to one side.

"Right, enough of the theatrics Martin. I'm here to talk about my case. No more games."

She hadn't brought one. Another test, it seemed, and I was growing rather tired of them.

"I've nothing to tell you. I'm not part of this and I don't know who to trust. Everywhere I go people are out to get me."

She didn't listen, just edged closer to me and placed her hand on my knee. My chest tightened.

"I've been hired to investigate a disturbing increase in courier fraud over the past six months. You're astute with that sort of thing, aren't you?"

Interesting. How would she know that? I hadn't said. Hannah? Had she sold me out? My pulse quickened as I reached for my collar, the scent of her strawberry shampoo bitter in my nose.

"Hannah has me to deal with large withdrawals. The customers can be sour, but the truth is often bitter."

Her notebook back in her hand, pen scratched away in my ears. Overbearing.

"The marked increase speaks to insider support, doesn't it? A member of staff with access aiding the fraudsters. That's our theory, anyway, but it's chillingly plausible, isn't it?"

Pulled at my collar as she stared at me, piercing my secrets with her eyes. I'd tell her nothing, still unclear whether she was friend or foe. For all I knew, she could report directly to Gary himself, the lemony little bastard.

"Yes. It does. It makes tactical sense. Evidence points to an inside man."

Bastard bloody bitter mouth! I breathed deep, closing my eyes, her hand warm atop my knee. Too warm, heat searing me. She was sizzling me atop a grill, melting out my secrets one at a time. Had to stay cool like Frank.

"Exactly. So, can you walk me through when things started to feel off? When did you first notice something different at the bank?"

All these questions, sharp, bitter daggers in my ribs. I needed her to stop digging.

"Lemons. Overtime. Get out."

Her smile faded.

"Oh but Martin, I was rather hoping to chat more. I'm so enjoying your company!"

She shuffled even closer to me, flicking back her beautiful, fiery red hair. Her eyes headlights, my heart racing. Leaned over. Lemons in my eyes. I wish William were here. I needed backup. Frank? No, Frank's a fridge. Nobody could help me now, and I only had one banana left. I got the feeling she was edging towards it and I needed her questions to cease.

"Citrus? Cheeseca—"

"Shhh."

Placed her finger over my lips and smiled at me. Popped her notebook to the side, and grinned wide.

"So... Just tell me something," she began, voice barely a whisper. "You'd be the first to notice anything amiss at the bank, right? Dealing with those big withdrawals?"

A fair comment, though her intensity had my sour heart beating out of my chest. Perhaps I would—it made logical sense.

"Unlikely. Hannah refers the customers to me and I help them."

She placed her arm around my shoulder, smiling at me, emerald eyes sharp against my souring walls.

"You've been very helpful, Martin. Keep this between us for now, won't you? Our little secret."

She leaned in even closer, kissed me on the cheek. Her lips felt like acid, her hand on my thigh like lava.

She sprung up from the sofa and winked at me, grabbing her coat from the rack nearby.

"Just one more question, Martin?" she said carefully, hovering by the door, myself in tow. "Are you seeing someone? I noticed a wedding ring, but no wife right? She left?"

My smile sank. Fell right off my face, flopped into a puddle on the floor.

Lesbian. Husband. Australia. Lemons. Jessica.

"She's gone. Left. Took my... Took my daughter. Took... Took everything."

The bitter tang of truth called tears from my eyes once more, acid on my cheeks. She rushed over and hugged me tight, her body warm and firm pressed against mine.

"You poor dear," she began, softly whispering in my ear. "Professional judgement can falter through traumatic times, can't it? Well, keep your wits about you. Let's do dinner."

Closed the door behind her and slumped against it. Somehow, the whole thing left a sour taste in my mouth. I lost something today, but I could only begin to imagine what.

Chapter 11

"It was true, William. All of it. You thought I was mad, citrus themed dreams and a ludicrous lost lemon cause. But I told you—lemons tell no lies."

He didn't respond, not yet at least. Just stood there smiling gently, no judgement, just compassion.

"Look, Marty. I'm worried about you. Ever since the uh... Incident? You've been chasing lemons like a lunatic. You need to talk to a professional, and accept the fact that you'll never see J—"

"NO!" I roared at William in a burst of citric fury. Sprayed sour saliva all over him. He tried to paw it off, but it was no use.

"Can't hide in the lemon trees forever, mate. At some point, they're fit to burst."

Was done listening to this. Between that creepy, gorgeous impersonator and my fraudster boss, I was tired. So tired.

Time passed once more, woke up on the sofa, room dark around me. Welcomed the break from the yellow, surrounded still by bitter lemons. The curtains, the walls, my soul.

Text had come in, checking my phone. Hannah.

"Just me, Marty. You feeling OK? Want some company tonight? Oh, and are you coming to work

tomorrow? You're still on a phased return, so just let me know."

Gibberish. Maybe I should try reading it again. Maybe I should wash the bitter taste of lemon from my mouth first.

Downed a glass of water, scratched against my throat. Spluttered, glass plonked on the table. Back to the message.

This text was no question. It was a threat disguised as one. She knew I was onto her, and wanted to come round and finish what she started.

I had no will to. I hadn't slept a full night since... Australia, and she wore me out in a long winded battle of the flesh last time. Thud, thud, thud.

The text message. A command, an order. Ask me how I feel so I let my guard down. Ask me to come over, because she wants to plant some evidence? The lemonade, still in the fridge. It mattered somehow.

I stared at the message again, my eyes welling, the bitter zest causing them to water. The mask slipped, the sour truth beneath the words sprang forth:

Just me.

Are you OK?

I want company tonight.

You're coming to work tomorrow.

You're still on my phase.

Let me know.

There it was. The truth, in all its bitter glory. She wasn't satisfied taking my family from me, she wanted samples of my future family too.

"Frank, mate?" I asked gently, showing him the text as he hummed away. "Am I being a tangy tart here? Or am I onto something?"

Silence. Stoic, stout, strong silence, just hummed away happily, ever watchful, ever vigilant. Seemed I'd have to consider my own course of action—Frank had enough lemons on his plate already.

Hoped he was OK. I did worry about him from time to time. I should get him some more of those business cards he likes, maybe a new fridge magnet or two.

Phone began to vibrate. Call incoming from Hannah. Took a deep breath, sat back down, and exhaled. Tap.

"Hey Marty. Sorry, I just wanted to talk. Saw you got the text and didn't reply. Really, are you OK?"

I couldn't honestly answer that. Life wasn't all bad— my family were missing, but I had my friends Frank and William watching over me. Had to admit, though, Frank was definitely my favourite.

"No. I'm not."

Starting to sour at this mouth of mine. Runs off on its own like a lemon rolling down a hill.

"Poor Marty. Come on, come over? We can cuddle and watch something on telly? Or better yet, not watch something?"

More coded messages. Dammit, Frank, I wish you could talk. Still, I wasn't in the mood to travel.

"I'd like that. I'll be there by ten."

"Yay! See you soon!"

Call ended with a click. Seems I've a mission tonight after all. Bones weary, eyes heavy. I needed to prepare.

Called the number, hand shaking. I wasn't going on a mission without backup.

"Pizza Palace?"

"Yes, I'd like some backup please. They're onto me."

Pause. Silence.

"Sir, you've called a pizza place? Would you like a pizza?"

"Oh! Very kind of you. Yes, please. Lemons."

"We're not putting lemons on pizza, bloody nutter. Now are you serious about ordering or not?"

"I have my orders. I've an investigation to complete. The lemons are listening."

"Swear everyone in this bloody town is on magic bloody mushrooms! You ordering or not?"

"Don't need any mushrooms, thanks. Frank has some I bought earlier."

Call ended with a click. Breathed deep, exhaled as I closed my eyes. Backup on the way, free pizza too. Couldn't wait.

Chapter 12

Couldn't show up to my mission tonight without protection. Popped into the corner shop, eyes on me. Cameras everywhere, shutters drawn on one of the windows. Convenience or control? Citrus or strawberry?

Shopkeeper smiled, offered me an awkward wave. Wonder what secrets hid behind those big brown eyes.

Found the shelf with the guns. Dozens of them, some riper than others. Found a firm one, nice and sturdy, as yellow as a banana. Or a lemon.

Elderly woman frowned at me, watching me inspect the guns. Judgemental. Hope she never needed one herself, a bitter burden to bear.

There we go. Sidearm, locked and loaded, ready to rock or roll. Bitter tang of lemons soured my sight, chilling in an orange netting nearby.

Gary in the fridge, too. They all had names, but I couldn't tell them apart. I could see a Michael or two in there somewhere. Fridge chilled me with a blast of air as I opened it, pulled out a box caging a Gary. This one was called 'Acidity Regulators' from glaring at the box. Stupid name for a sour tart.

"Sir? Everything is OK, sir?" shopkeeper questioned. Great, seems I've stumbled into another interrogation. Had to stay sharp.

"Guns, no millimetre. Need a sidearm for a dangerous mission tonight. Lemons."

Held my gun, checked the safety. Still intact, peel preserved. Shopkeeper laughed out loud, but only for a moment. His stare soon turned sour.

"Uhh... You buy this banana, sir?"

"Lemons."

"No sir, is banana. Sir, are you OK?"

Couldn't get the answer he wanted the first time, it seemed. Clutched at my collar, door dinging as another suspect entered.

"Marty! Fancy seeing you here. Dinner tonight, then?"

Juliet? Was she tracking me?

No, that made no sense. Her fiery red hair burned back the bitter citrus tide, firmly on my side. Yet my pulse quickened when I saw her, nerves tanging with zest.

"Marty?"

"No. Sorry. Got a mission tonight."

"Well, that sounds exciting! Does it involve a pack of bananas and a lemon cheesecake, then?"

"Most things seem to these days."

She giggled, trotting off to the wine shelf as I paid the shopkeeper for my munitions. His grin lied to my face, bitter, hiding fear. Had Juliet spooked him? Perhaps my fault, still holding my gun.

Holstered it in my pocket and headed out the door. Had a Gary, had a gun, had a bitter boss to visit.

Back home, equipment laid out on the kitchen table. Phone, guns, photo of Jessica.

"Frank, mate? I'm scared. Any last minute advice?"

Just hummed away happily. Maybe he's right. Just hum, relax, and stay sharp lest things turn sour.

Arrived at Hannah's in a blink. Barely remembered driving, may even have walked.

Door stood before me like some kind of wooden barrier between myself and the target. Gun felt heavy in my pocket, Gary steady in my other hand.

Approached and hovered my hand above the door, ready to knock. Something gave me pause. What if Hannah really, truly was the fraudster? And how, exactly, did it connect to the lemons?

Couldn't stay out here mulling over citrus conspiracies all night. Bitter chill, sour against my skin, dark of night above.

Stars were beautiful. Wonder if my family were gazing up at these same stars right now.

Didn't wonder long. Was early morning on the other side of the world. If that's where they even went.

Dropped Gary. Stamped on him, hard. His guts splattered across the pavement, the door bearing witness to my citrusy crime.

Breathed deep, closed my eyes. Got sloppy. Gary's guts all over the floor like a crime scene.

Scraped up as much of him as I could, chucked him in the bin outside. It was oddly dehumanising to hide the evidence like this. Did he have kids of his own? Hoped not.

Couldn't bear to think about it. Bitter chill of the late night gale robbing tears from my eyes.

Distracted myself long enough, and Hannah had been staring at me from the doorway for some time. Probably should say something.

"Um, bit of a cheesecake scenario. Situation, if you will."

Raised her eyebrow, arms crossed over her chest. "So I see. Come inside then. Got a banana for me?"

"Several."

Her smile wicked, her eyes piercing. Blue like the ocean, washing over the cracks in my armour. She was good, had barely said a word and already found my shoulders slumping, sighing and smiling from her sofa.

"You like my new dress? Thought you might find it 'a-peeling', get it?"

I didn't. It was yellow as the ripest of lemons, tang in my trousers as she modelled it in front of me.

"Lemons," I responded curtly.

"I'll get you some lemonade," she mumbled, shuffling off to her kitchen.

Was strange to see Frank here. Same model, same make, same colour. But her Frank was different, adorned with colourful fridge magnets.

Found myself stood next to Hannah, startling her as she turned around.

"Marty! I swear you're part cat burglar. So what was that you were saying? I do agree that it's a little strange."

Wait. What?

Lemons? No. No, not lemons. There was more. Bastard! What had I said?

"Remind me," I requested, cold glass of lemonade gripped tight in my hand.

"Lemons," Hannah may have said.

Fuck. Think I need to sleep. My thoughts turned sour, my focus fled.

Soon found myself on her sofa, something on the telly. Couldn't say what, hadn't heard a word. Time had passed, and I was somehow far more exhausted.

"Bathroom?" I asked.

"Oh, don't you remember silly? Second door on the left."

Remember? From when?

Dragged myself to my feet, approaching the hallway. Yet somehow I found myself approaching Frank's brother. Something had caught my eye, bitter sting of citrus in my sight. Lemons gripped at my throat as I touched the magnet, note pinned below.

"Dear Hannah,

Thanks again for your help. You've been a star.

From the other Hannah Stevens"

Pulse in my ears. The other Hannah Stevens? The... The courier fraud victim? But... What did this mean?

Room spun. Eyes ached. Rushed to the bathroom, washed out my eyes, time and time again. The sting remained.

What the hell did I just find? It mattered, it had to. I needed to stay calm, couldn't get distracted.

"Marty? Thought you'd got lost!"

Hannah stood outside as I pulled open the bathroom door. Hannah Stevens.

"No."

"Want to see something I think you might like?"

Interesting question. It gave me pause, opted not to answer.

"Sure."

Bastard mouth.

Followed Hannah to the next door down, grin on her face. Wicked, cruel or playful? Couldn't tell.

Her bedroom. Neat, tidy, except she'd left an article of clothing lying on top of her bed. Careless, messy.

"What do you think? You like it?"

Held it up against herself. It was a bright yellow corset, tang returning quickly to my hips. Stepped closer to her and sniffed her hair.

Clutched at my collar. "Lemons."

"Thought you might approve. Seems to match that dashing yellow suit you've been wearing, I thought."

Looked down, pawed at myself. White shirt, bright yellow tie, matching citrus suit. Was I the one working for the lemons all along? My citrus crusade aimed squarely at the man in the mirror?

Tired. Needed to go. Had to think of something, say something smart, sharp, final, get myself out of here.

"Would look better on my bedroom floor."
Oh fuck.

Chapter 13

Finally, back out into the night. That was exhausting, though I felt myself grinning ear to ear.

Not for very long, though. I was being followed—I was sure of it. I arrived home and headed inside, no lights, veiled by darkness.

Gun in my pocket. Ate two of the others, worked up an appetite.

Slipped out my back door, headed down the narrow dark alley beside my home to the front of the house. Scanned the area, see what I could find.

A figure. Sat in a nearby car, camera pointed my way.

Pulse quickened, heart pounding in my ears. They were onto me. The figure left the car and approached.

Hand in my pocket, gun at the ready. But no need—sighed deep, seeing it was Juliet, unmistakable fiery red hair.

But what the hell was she doing here? Why follow me? It had gone midnight.

She walked right up to me, zealous, zesty. Grabbed the back of my head and kissed me hard.

Chest tightened like a vice grip as she ran her hands through my hair. She pulled back and smiled, glow of the streetlight in her eyes.

"Why were you following me?" I asked deadpan, not skipping a beat.

"Isn't it obvious?" she replied, eyebrow raised. "I'm investigating. Saw you at Hannah's and I guess I got curious."

Suddenly, without warning, her hand on my banana.

"And jealous."

My hand shook a little. Her hypnotic eyes were soothing to stare at, fresh as a tangy glass of lemonade.

She gestured me inside. Time soon passed, found myself without my suit, sat next to Juliet on my sofa.

"Lemons," I said, phone out, pictures shown to Juliet.

"I see. I came to the same conclusion."

She buttoned up her shirt and hardened her gaze. Questions persisted.

"Tell me more about Hannah Stevens."

"Sweet old lady. Nearly fell victim to courier fraud."

"No, not her. Though, she did fall victim Marty. Later that same day, in fact."

Bastard. The lemon-scented losers got back in her head. Ten grand down the pan, sat in some fraudster's pocket.

"But we helped her. Hannah has a magnet on her fridge from her. A note."

"I see. Anything else?"

"Second phone."

Juliet writing in a notebook again, pen scratching, echoing in my ears. Hadn't even seen her bring it in.

"Well, been fun Marty. Think I have everything I need here. Try to sleep? You look shattered."

Kind of her to care, though Frank's humming seemed louder, more fervent than usual.

Juliet left, found myself alone on the sofa, sat in my lemon boxers.

It was very late. I found myself needing counsel. Really wanted to talk to William. Pulled out my phone.

"William mate, you there?"

"Hey, Marty. What time is it? Bloody hell, go to sleep!"

"Can't. I've got a problem."

"What's going on?"

Sat and talked it through with him. He didn't judge, just compassionately listened as I vented my bitter issues.

"You do realise you're stuck in a triangle now, don't you?" William said finally, after some pause.

I hadn't. Fuck.

Just want my daughter back, and for the bitter tang of lemon to leave my throat. Just want to sleep.

Yet found myself sat in the hallway, gun aimed at the door. Frank hummed away nearby, offering that stoic support I'd come to depend on. Long night on overwatch ahead.

Chapter 14

Barely slept. Up most of the night, guarding my door. Got fed up, no movement spotted. Decided to talk to Frank about my problems instead. I'd never met such a good listener, except maybe Janet. Hummed happily away as I spilled my guts to him, chest a little lighter.

Eyes much heavier, though. Was hard to remember the last time I'd properly slept. Pawed away at a cup of coffee, waiting at my desk, another exciting day of serving the British public soon to start. Already eyeing up my ethernet cable, imagining the sour conversations ahead.

Place had turned me a little bitter. Maybe it was time for me to move on, find a new lot in life. Couldn't exactly just ditch everything and go, though. My savings were gone. My family. My hope.

"Morning, Martin," Hannah said softly. "My office?"

Ah, I'd done something wrong again, it seemed. Or maybe she knew I was onto her? Juliet made it clear to me last night that Hannah was involved in the inner workings and dealings of this bank. She had every bit as much influence and pull as one would expect of a manager even.

To my mind, all but confirmed she was guilty. That and the lemon yellow dress she wore, accentuating her lemon yellow eyes.

Stared at them a little harder as she spoke. Shook my head. Blue. Blue eyes.

"So... How do you feel about that, Martin?"

Bugger. Found myself in her office, her words sour to my ears. Bitter tang of guilt lingered on her tongue, citrus in her yellow eyes.

"Lemons," I replied simply. Maybe.

"Well, we have to stay professional, despite all of that. Just... Keep this between us, OK? Nobody can know."

Nodded, excused myself. Rushed to the bathroom, shoved open the door with zest. Stared at myself in the mirror.

Almost didn't recognise me. Stubble-laden chin, bright hazel eyes, but that smile I wore turned sour, bitter taste of harsh, sharp citrus clawing at my throat. I close my eyes, and she's there. Her laugh. Her smile. Pushing her, on the swing, higher and higher. Too young to know what happened. Too young to care.

Eyes stung like someone smashed lemons into them. Tears washed away the bitter tang from my eyes. I found myself missing Frank somehow. His humming soothed the sour truth, rhythmic, mellow, yellow.

Yellow suit, tight, lemon tie clutching my throat. Bathroom stank of bitter citrus. Stepped back out, wiping my eyes and approached my desk. The adoring British public awaited patiently. Well, not so sure about that part.

"About time," the elder gentleman said. "Call this service? I've been waiting here for seven minutes!"

I'm sure he had important plans for those seven minutes. Daytime television, maybe feeding the ducks bread, possibly ranting at the newspaper. Who could say. Who could care.

Seven minutes he could rob from my quickly fleeting existence instead.

"Excuse me? I'm talking to you, young man!"

Not quickly fleeting enough.

"That's factually inaccurate, sir," I began. "I'm over thirty. Though I could see how that's young from your perspective."

His face turned sour, mouth agape, bitter zest of anger painted across his face.

"How... How dare you! I'll have you know, I fought in the war!"

"There have been many wars, sir," I began. "I'll assume you meant the Battle of Hastings, given your advanced age," I finished politely.

He stormed out, the woman behind him eyes open wide. Concerned, perhaps? By what?

Tie began to clutch at my throat, lemons scratching and scraping at my windpipe. They were watching. They were all watching, all judging, all plotting, all scheming. And Hannah was behind it all, yellow dress, lemon eyes.

"Next, please?"

"Uh, yes, thanks. I'm here to report fraud please. I've been the victim of fraud."

Hannah up to her tricks again? Lemons tell no lies.

"Let's go into the private room. Follow me."

Led her into the room and sat her down. She looked sour, bitter, broken. Eyes ablaze with yellow fury.

"So, what happened?"

"Yes. So I ordered two chicken burgers from McDonald's but I only got one. They refused to give me the other one, saying I hadn't ordered two. But there's two payments! I've been defrauded!"

This seemed serious. That was a 100% loss of funds, a staggering, bitter loss. Poor woman.

"Oh no, that's quite serious. Have you been to the police?"

Her gaze narrowed, sharpened.

"Um, no? Just refund me the money?"

"For a serious loss like this, you'll need a crime reference number."

"What!? It's like four quid! Just refund it!"

"I'm afraid there needs to be a proper investigation first, and we'll have to destroy your debit card. We'll order you a new one."

"What the hell are you talking about? I'm not giving up my card!"

"Ma'am I know this is scary, but to report serious fraud you must replace your card. It isn't safe to keep using it."

"Serious fraud!? It's a fucking chicken burger!"

"Yes, it represents a 100% loss of funds. That's a serious crime. You'll need to report to the police immediately before we can get involved."

"I'm not going to the police over a burger! Just refund it!"

"Have you tried interviewing the other burger? Perhaps it knows what happened to its friend."

She scraped her chair back and stood.

"Oh, I get it. You're making fun of me. Fuck you, bitter prick."

Seems she'd turned sour. Some people just weren't ready to accept that they were victims. Carrying that burden came with responsibilities.

Back at my desk, next adoring fan due. Fiery red hair, piercing green emerald eyes. Almost recognised her.

"Hi Marty!"

"Lemons."

She giggled. "I had fun last night too. You're unhinged, hungry, zesty. We'll have to do that again."

"How can I help you, ma'am?"

Her gaze narrowed, hands stuffed into her pockets. "Oh, um, I'm not here to see you actually. Need a word or two with—ah, there she is."

Hannah had been hovering nearby. Her face, painted with fury, sour at the sight of Janet.

Juliet. Sight of Juliet.

"I'm a busy woman, Miss Smith. What do you want?"

Hannah's arms folded across her chest like a shield. Secrets hidden in plain sight, eyes firmly locked on Juliet's throat. Her bitter scowl could pierce metal.

"Your office? Just a few minutes."

Juliet winked back at me, blowing a kiss as Hannah brushed invisible zest from her dress. There was a bitter, tart taste in my mouth from that whole interaction.

Found myself back in the side room, elder gent in front of me.

"Lemons."

"That's right! Said I'm to bring them the evidence. I'm working directly with the police—I'm special, don't you know."

"Police? Good. Police are serious, professional, and tactical."

"Absolutely. So I can withdraw the two grand?"

"Yes, of course. Just be sure to return with your crime reference number."

"Great! Thank you, young man. Our Majesty will thank us both for stopping these corrupt bastards."

"Excellent work."

Secured the man his evidence, handed him the bag. Off he went, back to his job working for the police as a special informant. Somehow, being a teller at a bank felt sour in comparison. Pit formed in my stomach. Envy? Bitterness? Didn't matter, it would soon pass.

Juliet winked at me, walking out, shortly in tow from the police informant with his bag of evidence. Hannah stood nearby, staring at me.

"My office. Now."

Heart skipped a beat, thudding in my ears. Zest in her words almost felt acidic as they rang in my ears.

Closed the office door behind me, Hannah's smile turned sour.

"Marty, in case it wasn't clear, I'm interested in pursuing you. Look, I know we've got to be careful because of work and...everything...but I want you to stop seeing Juliet."

How was that even possible? Did I have to close my eyes every time I spotted her now? Narrowed my gaze, tie felt like acid against my throat. Her words tart, eyes sour, lips bitter. She was hiding something, and I needed to know what.

"Lemons. Lemons, lemons, lemons."

Smile returned to her lips, as much as it did her eyes. More words were exchanged, but I didn't hear them, nor feel them leave my bastard mouth. I did feel hers against mine, though, zesty as a refreshing glass of lemonade.

"Keep your mouth shut, Marty. Until you're next round mine, anyway. Now go on, get your cute butt home."

Hannah giggled, beckoning me out her office door. Home it was, then, but something still felt sour.

Chapter 15

Sighed, slumping into my sofa back home. I barely blinked, yet here I was? There was a zing in the air, a refreshing waxy scent.

Pulled out my phone, scrolled to my gallery. Smile on Janet's face a bitter tang in my heart. Jessica's smile soured my resolve.

I was never going to see her again, was I? Eight billion people on this big blue ball. We were two of them.

Cried my eyes out, tears of acid stinging my cheeks. Somewhere out there, she was waiting for her Daddy, and the sour git didn't have a clue where.

Cruel. It was cruel, what Janet did. All of it. It still made no sense at all. I remembered the speech as though it were a script from a movie.

Met a woman. Lesbian. Husband. Lemons. Australia.

The words buzzed through my brain like a furious yellow wasp trapped by a window. He could see outside, but he'd never be able to reach it, not alone. Just like me. Just like Frank.

It was hard work, and my muscles were on fire, but I dragged one of the sofas into the kitchen. Sat by Frank and stared.

"Not keeping it together as well as I thought, am I Frank?"

He didn't judge, he just listened. Don't think I could have made it through all this without my constant companion, ever watchful, ever vigilant, guarding my home against Gary and his Lemon legion.

It still surrounded me. Yellow sofas, lemon wallpaper, lemon curtains, lemons, lemons, lemons. Janet loved the zingy little buggers, but the sour tang turned quickly to ash in my mouth. Nothing refreshing about the zest of betrayal.

"Brace yourself, mate. Just opening you up for a moment. Won't be long, I know it hurts."

Pulled open Frank, took a look inside. Gary, in his box, chilling away.

"Feel like confessing yet, Gary?"

Nope, silent as stoic Frank. Not even close to cracking.

Bags of lemons surrounded him. I'd been capturing them from the corner shop as and when they invaded the shelves, keeping them contained within Frank alongside their lemony leader.

Frank started to beep in agony, rhythmic sound of his suffering sour to my ears. Closed him up and placed my hand against his cool metal.

"Sorry, mate. Get some rest. You look tired."

Frank's hum seemed a little gentler than normal. Pulled off most of my suit, lay on the sofa with a blanket. Sound of Frank's humming finally put me to sleep.

Hours went by, in the blink of an eye. Checked my phone, it had gone seven in the morning. Didn't feel refreshed, exactly, but the rest had given me back some spark.

"Morning, Frank."

No reply, but never expected one. Not a chatty chap my Frank, but a firm friend. Never so much as moved, always stood sentinel.

Phone in my palm, looking for a friend. No Frank, but at least this one spoke back, when he could be bothered.

"Hey, William. Been a rough few days."

"So I see. What the hell happened, Marty?"

"Things are changing, and none of them are my choice."

William sighed. "Yeah. I get that. You look like shit, mate. Sorry to say it so plainly."

"Appreciate the honesty. I feel it, William. I just want my family back."

"Not going to find them, mate. Especially not dating two women. Didn't know you had it in you, sly old dog."

Hell was he talking about? Dating? Two women? Two chicken burgers. Two grand.

Fuck. FUCK. FUCK FUCK FUCK—

FUCKING LEMONY CUNTS—

FUCK!

"Marty? What's going on? You're freaking out, mate. Calm down!"

"TRICKED! CONNED! BITTER LEMON CUNTS!"

Threw my phone at the wall, smashing it to pieces. Took a bag of lemons out of Frank, cold snap of air meaningless against my fiery fury.

"YOU! You bitter little bastards. Tricked me. Scammed me. Conned me. Two thousand lemons! FRAUD!"

Heart pounding hard, chest tight with a sour citric rage.

Dropped them on the floor.

Stomped.

Stomped again.

Stomped some more until the bitter lemon bastards were splattered across my tiles like a bloody yellow crime scene.

Whole body shook, zesty tears of acid in my eyes. Stared down at my crime. Murder. Cold blooded, brutal, bitter murder.

Dropped to my knees, scrubbing with a sponge. The air smelt so fresh, tart, the citrus tingle of trampled lemons. Lemons who had their own families, their own friends, and their leader.

Gary. Gary the lemon fucking cheesecake.

Sat there in his box, laughing at me, witness to my crime. The bitter rage soon deflated into a sour sadness. He would have his vengeance, I was sure.

No matter how hard I scrubbed, the evidence remained. Air stank of it. Tiles looked so clean, fresh.

Never before in my life had I ever let bitter rage consume me so completely. Left a hollow tang in my chest, a sour smile curled towards the tiles below.

Slumped on the sofa, stared at the wall and the remnants of my former phone crumpled in a heap on the carpet. Another victim of the citric crusade, caught in the crossfire.

Nothing for it. Sighed deep, dragged myself to my feet. Lemon suit adorned, camouflaged and ready to go.

Walked into the town centre. Eyes, everywhere, dozens and dozens of them. Two per person, typically.

"Welcome, sir, how can we help?" the cheery young lady said as I pushed my way into the phone shop. Not a single lemon-haired insurgent in sight. I was safe here.

"I'm sorry. So sorry."

Presented my shattered phone to her. She carefully took it from me, and set it on her counter.

"Oh dear! It's OK. What happened?"

"Another victim of the citric crusade. Lemons can be ruthless."

She giggled. Perhaps her way of handling serious grief. She would have to let his family know, after all. Couldn't be an easy job.

"Right, well, you got a warranty on this thing?"

"No, though I do know a chap called Warren who does love a good cup of tea. Does that count?"

Raised her eyebrow, smile turned sour. "Um, no? What kind of phone are you looking for to replace it, then? Can we do you a deal?"

"Yes, I know a guy called Adeel too. Devout Muslim. Insightful chap, if a bit rigid at times. Haven't seen him in twenty years, though."

Giggled again. She wasn't taking the fall of the phone too well at all. Poor girl.

"Are you some kind of stand-up or something? You're hilarious! Charming, too, in that yellow suit."

Some camouflage this turned out to be.

"No, I much prefer sitting down."

More giggling, tangy to my ears. Relented and smiled back myself.

"Well, what kind of phone do you want?"

"Yes, please. I'll have a kind one. The more compassionate the better."

"OK! Stop making me laugh or we'll be here all day!"

"No, you close in two hours."

This was going terribly. Had never seen someone deflect with so much giggling before. She needed to be brave.

"How about this one? It's a more modern version of your crumpled friend there."

Crumpled, shattered, defeated. Replaced by a newer, better model. Australia.

"Sir? Ready to sign a contract, then?"

"Oh, no can do. My wife would kill me."

She chuckled a little, though it didn't meet her eyes. The zing behind them was gone.

"Sign here, please."

I didn't know any sign language, so I just wrote my name instead.

"Thanks Mr Fletcher. Enjoy your new phone!"

"Yes, thank you. Once again, my condolences."

Stepped out the store, new phone, headed home.

Stopped off at the corner shop first, got the rest of the ingredients I'd need for my mushroom lemon risotto. Been too long since I had a delicious meal, and those celebrity mushrooms still sat waiting in Frank.

Charged the phone a while, staring at it. Seemed to work just fine.

"Sorry about earlier, William."

"That's alright. You've been through a lot. What happened?"

Good question. What had happened? I could barely remember. Something to do with fraudulent lemons.

"The number two. Angered me, for some reason."

"You lost the two most important people in your life. Understandable, Marty."

"They're not lost, they're in Australia."

"Marty, not what I mean. They're not coming ba—"

Slammed the phone down on the sofa. Resisted the sour urge to pelt it at the lemon coated wallpaper like last time. Already had to remarry to get this one. I'm sure Hannah would be happy about that.

Scooped cereal right out the box. Didn't bother with the lemonade. Tasted bitter, sour tang in my mouth.

Call came in. Hannah.

"Marty..." cleared her throat, audibly sighed. "I need to see you in my office. Can you come in today, please? Immediately if you can."

Felt like a trap. Lemons clutched at my throat as I tried to respond.

"Lemons."

"Great. See you soon, Marty."

She sounded cold, professional, tactical. Bitter, even. Something had her spooked.

Finally realised I was onto her and her little lemon conspiracy, it seemed. Fine, she'll have her little meeting, but I'll not go unarmed. Touched the smooth skin of the gun in my pocket as I headed to the bank.

Chapter 16

Bitter tang of eyes, sharp stares, lemons everywhere. Walking past a charity shop and I saw it.

Yellow fabric called to me. Pushed open the door, headed inside.

"Morning sir, how can I—"

"Tactical headgear, lemon-scented. Undercover mission. Have you tested the operational effectiveness?"

"Uh... What?"

"Lemons."

Her mouth agape, staring. Tang in the air, citrus clawing at my throat.

"Sorry sir, I don't understand. It's just a balaclava, for winter weather. They do wear them in the army, but I think black ones, not bright yellow ones like this."

It was beautiful, and military approved. I had to have it. Pulled out my wallet, handed it to her.

"Uh, thanks. OK, enjoy your new balaclava, dear."

"Already eaten, sorry."

Nodded and left, smile zesting my lips. Didn't much enjoy baklava anyway. Tang in my step on the walk back home, eager to show my acquisition to my best mate.

"Frank, mate. Keep this safe for me?"

Stuck the baklava in his tummy, chilling with Gary and the lemon legionnaires. Finally some proper gear. Felt tactical, professional. Lemon legion wanted a fight? I'd make sure it turned sour.

Gave Frank a nod as I headed back out again. Needed to go to the bank and see Martin.

Hannah. Same thing.

Pushed open the door, fresh citrus scents acid in my nose. Perfume? Floor cleaner? Those zesty new adverts with the 'Freshest Savings rates in town!'

All lies. Half a percent behind the market leader. Lemons never used to lie, but something felt different.

"Marty."

Hannah's expression sour, eyes bitter. Beckoned me to her office once more. Starting to wish I'd brought my tactical gear, eyes sharp as they pierced my throat.

"Martin, there's been a serious incident of fraud."

Her expression lacked zing, her lips curled to her toes.

"Yes, I know. I warned her to go to the police, but she wouldn't do it. 100% loss of funds."

Hannah raised an eyebrow. "What's this? I'm talking about courier fraud, Marty. Two thousand pounds."

Wait.

Two chicken burgers.

Two grand.

Two thousand lemons.

FUCK!

FUCKING COURIER FRAUD! FUCK! FUCK! FUCKING LEMONY BASTARDS!

FUCK!!!

Smashed my fists onto the desk, slapped her notebook against the wall. Clawed at my eyes. They burned, acid, citric. Lemons. Lemons clutching at my eyes my throat my heart—

"Marty! Calm down!"

Her eyes, yellow. Her skin, yellow. Her hair, lemons. Lemons.

Shook my head, bitter zest piercing my ears. Ringing. Zinging.

Sour tears sank down my bitter cheeks. They got me. Bastard lemons got me. Two thousand pounds sterling, lost, all because she didn't go to the police over her chicken burgers. Fool.

Hannah gently placed her hand on my shoulder as I sobbed, kneeling, eyes burning like acid.

"Marty. I'm here. What happened?"

Wiped the bitter tears from my eyes. Would that I could wipe them from my heart.

"Lemons. Bastard, fucking lemons."

Hannah sighed. "It's... Not your fault. But there will be questions. You'll be suspended pending an investigation. I'm sorry, Marty. Just stick to what I told you, OK? Can you repeat that for me?"

"Lemons."

Hannah nodded, smile returning to her face. "Exactly right, word for word. Please, go home and get some rest. And I want you to see a counsellor as soon as possible. I'm worried about you."

Left her office more confused than when I'd entered it. I had no place on the council. Bitter fool like me? Not leadership material.

Eyes all over me as I walked home. Two thousand chicken burgers, gone. And it was my fault.

I needed Gary to crack, and soon. Preferably before me, sour citrus clawing at my throat.

"William, mate. I'm suspended."

"Oh Marty. I'm so sorry. Mate, what happened?"

Glared at my phone. "I don't really know. I think I messed up, mate. Lemons turned me sour."

"Marty, you need to do what Hannah says. She's got your best interests at heart."

"How can you know? You don't...you don't understand."

"Of course I do. You need to accept that your family isn't—"

"NO!"

Where the fuck was I? Found myself on a train, gun in my pocket. No tactical headgear, no backup. Wanted to go home. Didn't know where home even was anymore.

Lesbian. Lemons. Australia. Lemons. Jessica.

Lemons.

Chapter 17

"She did what? That bitch!" Juliet said, apparently sat across from me in the apparent restaurant I apparently found myself in?

"Lemons."

"Must admit, Marty... Her telling you to stay away, well... It's working for me," Juliet whispered, lemons nearly on full display as she flashed me a wicked grin.

Food arrived. Lemonade, fish and chips with a slice of lemon. Bitter end for a sour citrus crusader.

Felt refreshing to squeeze him dry. Fresh lemon scent adorning my fried fish, sour juice refreshing on my skin.

Practically tore the meal apart like a rabid lion tearing apart a lemon, Juliet laughing. Apparently she hadn't seen a lion before.

Train ride felt distant yet present. This restaurant had lemon wallpaper, exactly the same as the one in my living room, except it was brown without the lemon pattern. It was no coincidence.

"So that's kind of where I'm at, Marty," Juliet finished.

Not that I'd heard her start. Bloody lemons.

"Does Hannah know I'm onto her?" I lemoned with a grin.

Oh. That seemed a little too tactical for my tastes. Trying that again.

"Lemons."

"I don't know, but I think you should stay away from her, Marty. Besides, I'm much more fun anyway, right?"

Cackled like a sour, refreshing glass of lemonade. Tinged against my throat as I drank it down.

Head felt fuzzy. Like a leaky pen sat in my pocket, staining it from yellow to green, but in my head. Buzzing, bitter brain. Betrayed me, just like my bastard mouth.

"There's got to be a reason Hannah trusts you so much with all these fraud cases, Marty. What's so special about you?"

"Martin Fletcher, lemontieunant first class, badge number 73M0N."

"I swear your sense of humour doesn't make any."

Didn't make any what? Lemon pie? Lemonade? Gary?

Gary. That bitter little bastard. Two thousand chicken burgers and all he could do was chill in my Frank.

He had to crack soon. Needed him to. The bitter, laughing lemons were close. I could smell them. Hear them. Taste them as they clawed at my throat.

Maybe that was just the lemon fish.

"So come on, Marty. You're being quiet. When did you first start noticing the increase in courier fraud? Why did Hannah always assign them to you?"

"Lemons, lemons, lemons."

Leaned back in her chair, arms folded across her lemons. "Well, makes sense. But I need to know more, and you need to tell me. Someone is lying to me. You wouldn't lie to me, would you, Marty?"

Sour question. Pulse quickened, tugging at my collar. No way.

"Yes."

Juliet cackled, emerald eyes sparkled as her grin met her eyes. "Least you're honest about it. But what else aren't you being honest with me about, Marty? What secrets are you hiding?"

"Lemons tell no lies."

"Yeah. I'm starting to get that."

Pawed at her burger some more. Lemon meringue for dessert, bill came due.

"I need you to remember what I told you, Marty. I'm counting on you."

Not a word.

"Every word."

"Good boy. Now get me out of here, I'm bored, and feeling territorial."

Chapter 18

Woke up nearly feeling rested for once. First time in a long time.

Juliet left, long night of tactical training completed. Certainly worked up an appetite.

Suspended. Nowhere to go, nothing to do. Figured it was time to cook something proper.

"Frank, mate, you still got those mushrooms I bought from the celebrity chef?"

No reply. Didn't expect one. Didn't need one, could just check. Bitter twit.

Took out a captive lemon, placed him on the cutting board.

"You've taken everything from me. Time to talk, Gary."

Silence.

"Fine. You made this happen. This is on you."

Hand shook. Steadied it and cut the lemon clean in half. Bitter.

Stared at it a long while, citric stench of murder sour in my nose.

Took some doing, but my mushroom lemon risotto was finally ready.

"Cheers, Frank. Might finally feel better after some good food."

Texture was a bit odd, but it was delicious. Leftovers for tomorrow, too. Sat down on the sofa, smile on my face.

Sour pit in my stomach. No, a twist. No, a thought. It was thinking but I couldn't hear it.

Lemons on the wallpaper started to wobble. Had to stay sharp. Clearly tired, but maybe that was understandable given the two thousand lemon burgers and Hannah sleeping with Juliet.

No, that was all wrong. Jumbled up like a jumble sale, all sorts of curios and knick-knacks. What's a knick-knack anyway? Something bone related, probably. Dog called Paddy.

Wonder if you could get a funny bone transplant. Might need to give one to William, bitter bugger, all business. Never once seen him smile.

Or Frank, humming away there to himself. Boring bastard.

"Oi, Frank! Say something ya git!"

"Nah mate, don't feel like it. Besides, just a fridge mate," Frank responded.

"Fair enough. Enjoy your humming then mate."

"Will do. Hum-dee-dum-hum-hum."

Bless him. Still wouldn't talk, the stoic, stern, sour bastard. Loved him all the same. Handsome chap for a fridge, actually. A nice bright purple, really accentuated the lemons around him, on the walls, on the curtains, in my eyes.

Lemons started giggling, just a little. I think, anyway. Sort of hazy. Was that one dancing? Did that one wink at me? Sorry little lemon, don't zing that way.

Counted my fingers, just to make sure they were all still there. Couldn't have any mutineers on me, not with such an important mission ahead of me. Maybe it was time to talk to William.

Tried to, anyway. The phone wobbled, or was that my hand? Seemed to blur a little as it moved. Swear that lemon just blinked at me. What are they giggling about anyway? Maybe I need my own funny bone transplant, just didn't get the humour.

That or they were just being sour gits? Maybe Frank can translate for me. I'm sure he speaks lemon.

"Lemons don't laugh. Shut the fuck up already."

Seems they didn't want to listen. I shouldn't have been surprised, they didn't have any ears. Lemons were groves in plural. Or is it plurality? That feels better. That's the one. Lemon groves in their droves, dancing on the wallpaper. I could taste them, bitter tang of citrus on my tongue as I licked my lips.

"Oh! William. There you are."

"Marty? What the hell is going on? You look... Wrong, mate."

"Yeah, I think so. I still passed though. I'm not great at maths so I got at least half the questions wrong."

"No! Wrong, wrong. I'm not talking about any test."

"Love a bit of zest. Lemon rind scraped right over my risotto. Tasted like risotto, much to my surprise, just a bit more risottoey."

"Marty, please go sit down. Maybe call an amb—"

"Amber? Oh Marty, that takes me back. Never forget your first girl, do you mate? Remember Sophie? Sweet girl. Married now, surgeon. Done well for herself. Lovely lemons!"

"Frank, please go sit down. You're acting lemons."

"More of a bananas guy myself, mate. Prefer the sweet to the sour. Seems life has been nothing but sour lately."

Hadn't been paying attention as the lemons surrounding me grew louder. The giggles and snickers started to sound like laughter, only softer, and bitter to the touch.

The yellow was everywhere. I could hear it. Reached out and touched a dancing lemon on the wall, and it giggled. Then it started pointing. Pointing, and laughing.

"Hey... Pack it in. Not funny."

Didn't listen to me. Just kept pointing. Laughing. Pointing. Laughing.

Didn't have to listen to this bitter bollocks. Back to my sofa in the kitchen, sit with my buddy Frank. Oh, I forgot to say hello to William. And goodbye. And purple electric unicorn toaster sandwich, didn't say that either.

Didn't matter. Had time to eat the words later, maybe drink a few instead. Did find myself thirsty, the bastard lemons clawing at my throat.

"Frank, mate, you finally gonna talk?"

"Nah mate, sorry. I can't. I'm a fridge."

"Understandable. Getting pretty lonely round here, though. I miss my family."

"Yeah, makes sense. I'd love to talk to you about it, really I would, but I'm still just a fridge mate. Sadly fridges don't talk."

"Oh! That's not true, actually! I saw it on the news Frank. There's this smart fridge, orders stuff for you, says things to you. Lets you know when you're low on milk or lemons."

"Pretentious bastard. Bet he went to a posh school, the git."

"Hah! Yeah! Well, let me know if you ever feel like talking, Frank. I'll be here."

"Will do, but don't hold your breath mate. I'm still just a fridge."

"And fridges can't talk. Right. Thanks for being a good listener anyway, Frank."

"Course mate. Been with you nearly as long as your wife was."

"Yeah. You're a good guy, Frank. Really wish you could talk."

"Me too, mate. Sorry—still just a fridge."

"Just a fridge."

Curled up on the sofa a moment. Room spun as the lemons started dancing, glowing, singing laughing pointing. Little bastards didn't know when to shut the fuck up. Tired of the bitter little buggers turning my life sour.

Light from inside Frank started to glow like some kind of light. His hum turned sour, bitter, a tang of pain to it. Louder. I could taste his anxiety. Never expected anxiety to taste like strawberry, but guess it did make sense.

Reached out my hand, trying to hold Frank's handle.

"I'm here mate. What's wrong? What's happening?"

"Sorry, mate. Can't tell you because I can't talk—I'm still just a fridge."

"No, mate. You've been more loyal to me than my own bitter bitch of a wife. You're not just an anything. You're my best mate. Now come on, tell me what's wrong."

"Gary."

Frank seemed pained. Glow intensified. Could taste lemon with my eyes.

Pulse in my ears. Heart my mouth. Shoe on my foot. Something was happening. Something sincerely citrus.

Hand shook, cool metal of Frank's handle beneath it, ready to pull.

"Marty, mate, I know I'm a fridge and can't talk but seriously, buy a guy dinner before you crank his handle?"

Snapped my hand away. "Bugger. Sorry, Frank. Didn't mean to eat boundaries."

"Yeah, all good. Ugh, I don't feel so good."

Frank's humming got louder. Clearer, rhythmic. Almost sounded like Morse code. Not that I'd know what it meant, drank that textbook years ago. Didn't hear a word.

The glow intensified. Frank looked pained.

"Frank, mate? You alright?"

"Fridges don't talk mate. Urgh!"

Something was causing Frank pain. That lemony little tart in his box? Right. Sorry about cranking your handle, Frank—bitter little bastard needed to learn some manners.

Time to interrogate a cheesecake, and fast, before the bitter bugger murdered my Frank.

Chapter 19

Hand on Frank's handle. Didn't even buy him dinner first. Sorry mate.

Cranked it hard, Frank making a satisfying pop as he flew open and HOLY FUCK!

Dived for cover behind my sofa as the fucking CITRUS CRUSADE burst forth from Frank's mouth!

Fuck! I was surrounded!

Heart pounded in my ears. Lemons, everywhere, some laughing, others laughing, some even just pointing, laughing.

The lemon legionnaires poured from the fridge. Citric cannons in hand, lemon plated armour, ready for war.

And there he was.

Brilliant, floating, glowing lemon bastard.

"Gary."

"Pleasure, mate," Gary began. "You ready to finally bloody listen to me yet?"

Fuck did that mean? I'd been trying to get the bitter bastard to spill his juice for weeks.

The lemons were everywhere. Pointing, laughing. Others with their cannons trained on me, ready to fire.

Bitter, citric tears cascaded down my face as I cowered behind the sofa. More and more lemon legionnaires spilled from Frank's gaping maw. He started to rhythmically beep, clearly in pain.

Wasn't about to let my boy suffer. Can't let you down, Frank, like I did my Jessica.

Dived for my armoury, Gary grinning at me. Tactical headgear worn, guns in hand, and back behind the sofa as the citric crusaders began to fire.

Lemony blasts struck the sofa, juice everywhere. Bitter tang filled my nose, my eyes, my heart.

"Fuck you, Gary, and fuck your entire citric crusade!"

Lemon legion surrounded me. More and more of the bitter buggers poured forth from Frank with every passing moment.

Fury filled my chest, heart pounding in my ears. Popped up out of cover and opened fire, banana blaster in each hand.

Shot a couple lemons, citric explosions, juice everywhere. Bitter sprays of lemon assaulted me from the crusaders, flanking my position.

I was ready for them. Rolled out from cover and opened fire, blasting a dozen of them. The sound of explosions and lasers and lemons echoed through my skull.

"Can't fight me forever, mate," Gary mocked, floating near Frank, still beeping in pain. "I'll cram the bitter truth down your throat one way or another."

"NO!" I roared like a dinosaur, retreating to my living room, blasting lemons as they swarmed from Frank's mouth.

FUCK! One got me in the leg. Fucking stung, but the wound was superficial. I could still fight.

Cowered behind the armchair as more lemon legionnaires poured forth. Many pointing and laughing, many battle hardened crusaders.

Gary seemed to grow in tune with my fear. He could taste it, sour and salty like the sunrise.

"Please, just surrender Gary! This war can't go on forever!"

"You're right, it can't. Lemons! Advance!"

They rushed my position. Dozens and dozens of them. I dived behind the coffee table, narrowly avoiding a blast to the chest, gunning down dozens of the little bastards.

Big one pushed past, tactical gear, lemon grenades. Ears rang as they exploded in a burst of citric fury nearby. Shot him right through the lemon, others crowding him as he bled out on the carpet, sour citrus staining it.

Needed a plan. More of the big buggers swarmed forth, grenades flying everywhere. Tossed one of my guns out into the hallway, distracting the legion just long enough to close Frank and take cover behind my kitchen sofa once more.

"Frank, mate!" yelled above the chaos and the blasting. "You good!?"

"Still just a fridge mate! Can't talk!" Frank yelled back as lemon blasted everywhere, cannons barely missing my chest.

I was kneeling in a bitter pool of sour citric blood. The reinforcements had stopped, and only a fraction of the legion remained.

"Give it up, Gary. You're outgunned. I prepared for this—you can't beat me!"

"Can't not, mate. You lost the moment you saw your first lemon. You just don't know it yet."

"Fuck you!"

Popped up from behind cover, blasting the rest of his Lemon legion. Took another sour shot to my shoulder, bitter agony, tang of pain.

Heart racing. The legion all but dead, stragglers and Gary remained.

"Give it up, Gary!"

"Janet. Jessica. Lemons."

"FUCK YOU GARY! CITRIC CUNT!"

Popped out from the sofa, blasting the—

NO! Fucking gun was DRY!

FUCK!

"Seems you're spent, mate," Gary mocked. "You finally ready for the bitter truth?"

"FUCK OFF! I'M NOT DONE YET!"

Tossed my gun at Gary, nimbly dodging it with a bitter grin on his face. I'd prepared for this.

One big lemon legionnaire left, hidden behind Frank. Took another shot to my arm, tang of pain zesting my nerves, but I got it, blasted him same as the zest.

Wielded the banana like a hilt and focused. Feel the citrus, Marty. The zest is with you. Through the lemons, all things are possible. Be at one with the tang.

Brilliant beam of golden light erupted from firm yellow hilt.

"Give it up, Gary. The zest is with me, not you."

Swung my bananasabre, cleaving the remaining two of Gary's legionnaires in half, both hiding in the kitchen sink.

"Sorry, Marty. I'm just getting warmed up. Showtime."

Gary glowed bright, the sight loud in my eyes. Ringing in my ears as he summoned the fallen citric crusade in their entirety to himself.

They enveloped him, wrapped around him, giving him form. He was terrifying, the ultimate citrus crusader, adorned with waxy plate armour.

Heart pounded in my ears, eyes on Gary. Four arms, each one wielding a piercing, gleaming lemonsabre. Fuck.

"I'm willing to skip this whole fight right now, Marty. Truth is bitter, needn't be painful too."

My golden blade flickered for a moment. Citric cunt was in my head, trying to force me to drop my guard.

"No. Never. NEVER!"

Swung my blade in a downward arc, zestily blocked by Gary. All four of his Lemon blades thrusted back, barely dodged them in time.

"Give it up, Marty! You can't win!"

"You turned them against me!"

Our blades met, sparking, spitting, citrus in my eyes. Muscles full of acid, straining against his force.

"No, Marty. You did that yourself."

"NO!"

Swung for him again, cleaving one of his arms clean off. Bitter bastard regrew it almost instantly.

"Can't fight the truth forever, Marty."

"I HATE YOU!"

Swung furiously at Gary, sweeping, arcing, blade gleaming as it met with his.

"You were my brother, Gary! I loved you! Janet loved you, and I loved her!"

"Truth is often sour, Marty. You're going to hear it, if we have to fight to the bitter end."

Swung high, arms aching, chest pounding, sweat burning. Every blow, Gary intercepted seamlessly. I was outmatched, but I wouldn't give up. Couldn't. For my daughter. For Frank. For Marty.

Pushed me back against the wall, his blows furious, unrelenting. Four blades working in tandem, bitter barrage of citric fury. Sharp, sour stab of pain in my chest, banana flopped to the floor. Lemonsabre through my heart.

Coughed, spluttering lemon juice all over the carpet. Dropped to my knees, bitter tang of pain pulsing through my chest.

"I'm sorry, Marty. Really."

"Bitter cunt," I managed, curled up on the floor, lemon at my throat, in my eyes, in my heart.

Shook on the floor. Bitter tears stolen from my sour eyes.

Gary discarded the fallen, and hovered nearby. He seemed almost gentle now, the sharp, tart warrior who bested me seemed like a lifetime ago. Or a minute, wasn't really sure.

"The truth was hidden in plain sight all this time, Marty. You've seen it."

Couldn't hear it. Wouldn't hear it. Didn't hear it.

"Yeah, you can. You did. Janet's journal, lemon printed cover. Got that for her years ago, Christmas stocking gift, didn't you? She loved it. She loved you, too, Marty. But love can turn sour, bitter truths hidden in written words."

Nope! Didn't hear or read a word! Not one! No, nope. No.

"Yeah. You did. You saw it at the bottom of her wardrobe, when you tried her dress on. Very fetching, by the way, not a limp banana in sight."

"Why should I listen to you, Gary? With everyone out to get me, how do I know you aren't too?"

"Not everyone mate," Gary began. "Just that private investigator, your boss, your ex wife, me—"

"Janet? What's she got to do with this?"

"Like I said, journal, wardrobe, whatever. Sharpen up mate. Later."

Bitter little bastard, but... Lemons tell no lies.

Chapter 20

Woke up on the sofa, exhausted. It was gone midday. Throat dry, stomach sour.

Bedroom. Wardrobe. Journal.

There it was, at the bottom, just like Gary said. Felt like I'd been here before, hand on the lemon-printed journal.

Took it to the kitchen, sat on the sofa.

"Frank, I can't open this. Just looking at it twists my stomach in knots. What do I do?"

No reply. Couldn't expect one, him being a fridge, but his silence spoke volumes.

Oh. Lemons, lemon juice, splattered remnants of citrus zesting the air. This would be a bastard to clean up. What the fuck happened?

Phone out. "William, mate, you there?"

"Yeah Marty—whoa, the fuck happened in your kitchen mate?"

"Citric crusade. It was war. Bitter, sour war."

"Uh... Right. Well, I see you're holding a journal there. Looks important. What's in it?"

Journal suddenly felt hot in my hand, acid against my skin. Bitter tang of loneliness poked at my ribs. Memory of the playground, the swing, shook from my head.

"The truth. The bitter, sour truth."

"You need to read it. But first, you look like shit Marty. When's the last time you even had something to eat?"

"Mushroom lemon risotto. Don't honestly know. Could be an hour, could be an eternity."

"Right, well, get cleaned up, get some food in you, and I'll be here when you're ready to talk. You'll be alright, mate."

"Thanks, William."

Phone away, yellow rubber gloves on.

"Well, wish me luck Frank. Got some cleaning to do."

Time passed, minutes stretching as I scrubbed and scraped and cleaned. Worked up an appetite, scoffed the leftovers.

Seat on the sofa, journal in my hand. It was time. Hand was shaking like a lemon as I opened it.

Four tally marks on the inside cover. What did they mean? Decided to add a fifth. Somehow, it made sense. Bitter, sour sense.

Flicked through it. Found a script. An exit script, detailing a cascade of shocking events to an inevitable powerful conclusion. Lesbian. Husband. Australia. Jessica.

A message.

'Dear Marty,

Just wanted you to know how pathetic you are. I loved you for the longest time, but watching Hannah fuck you with her eyes got to me. She looked at you the way you looked at your daughter, nothing but unconditional love.

I got jealous. When she made you go to work events or stay late, I was sure she was going to make her move. Doesn't matter whether you did or not, I'd convinced myself you were cheating and it turned me sour.

Opportunity arose to get my own back. Fraud ring headhunted me, got one over on Hannah. I loved it. I loved all the tales you brought home of the fraud you stopped, whilst sneaking past bigger scores right under your nose.

Made sure to drain our joint savings account and implicate you, too. I'll be long gone before anyone knows I'm involved. Probably shouldn't have written this, but I just wanted you to know how much I hate you, and how happy I am to be starting a new life with my daughter.

Go fuck Hannah, and yourself,

Janet'

Shook. Convulsed. Tears, clawing, biting, bitter acid. The words seemed to leap up off the page, pointing, laughing. Lemons on the cover, pointing, laughing. Lemons on the walls, on the curtains, pointing, laughing.

Everyone. Everything. Pointing. Laughing.

"But not you, Frank. Frank. Please. Help me."

"Sorry mate. Just a fridge, can't talk."

Fuck.

How could Hannah do this? Why would she write a confession in a lemon-printed journal and plant it on her visit?

Was she truly that bitter?

And the script! The exact script that Janet used to shatter my world, to steal my savings, my daughter, my everything. Right there, written in the journal, like some kind of script.

Hannah. Bitter, sour Hannah. Coached Janet just like she coached the courier fraud victims. The lemons lied. But lemons tell no lies.

Tactical lemon suit equipped, tie fastened. Lemon-scented balaclava, military grade, adorned. Banana locked and loaded. Next the lemon grenades, sausages and journal.

This ends today.

"Open up, Frank. Need the rest of my gear mate."

Pulled Frank open. Grabbed a bag of lemons, military grade fragmentation devices. Pulled out the small green pin from the top of one and tossed it at the wall.

Exploded in a bright, zesty burst. The lemons on the wall began to cry citric, salty tears. Good.

"Get used to it, bitter little bastards. You'll be mourning more of your brothers by the time this is all over."

Tucked a couple sausages into my side pockets, too, just as planned. Might need the leverage.

"Frank, mate. Keep the house safe for me. Might not make it back from this one."

"Will do, Marty. Still can't talk though mate."

Lemons tell no lies, but the bitter little bastards certainly can die.

Chapter 21

Lemons, lemons everywhere. Pointing and laughing as I shifted from cover to cover on the approach to the bank.

Eyes upon me on the approach, but they didn't make a move. Tactical gear must have been intimidating, people crossing the street to avoid me.

Chest tight, bank in sight. Deep breath. Showtime.

Kicked the door open, tossed in a grenade. Gun held high in the air, journal in my pocket, heart in my ears.

"Everyone get down! This is a stick up!"

Blasted off a couple shots into the ceiling, get their attention.

All eyes on me. Old man starts chuckling.

"Bloody hell, sonny. You give us a right fright, bloody prankster. You gonna eat that banana?"

"No! But you are, if you don't get down! DOWN ON THE GROUND!"

His smile soured. Finally took me seriously, it seemed.

"You... You feeling OK, sonny?"

"Everyone get down! NOW!"

Tossed out a few more grenades as people rushed out the bank. Old man shuffled off, I threw another grenade. More explosions.

"Sir, seems to be the problem h—Marty? That you?"

The teller knew me, it seemed. Think I'd seen him before. Marvin? Matthew? Martin? Something like that.

"Get me your manager! Move!"

Fear zested his eyes as he shuffled off to the beast's lair. Fetch her, fool. Let's finish this.

Hannah rushed over, bitter concern tanging her eyes. "Marty? What the hell? What's going on?"

"As if you don't fucking know! Open the vault, let my family out! NOW!"

Fired my banana blaster as lemon legionnaires spilled from my bag of grenades. Bugger!

They soon began to swarm and multiply, the lights turning to lemons, the lemons turning to lemons.

Sirens outside, Hannah and MatthewMartinMarvin cowering behind cover.

They had backup, it seemed. Rushed to the door, blasting the legionnaires out the way.

"Back off! I have sausages!"

"Sir, nobody needs to get hurt. What's going on?"

"I'm serious! I have all the evidence right here! Back off or my sausages get it!"

"Sir please, no need to hurt anyone. Calm down. Are you armed sir?"

"Yes! Gun and grenades! You'll taste them if you don't back off!"

Time passed. Seconds? Years? Couldn't tell. More lemon legionnaires arrived outside, armed with shotguns and a megaphone. They got to the police. Lemons really were everywhere.

The walls pulsed and vibrated in time with the flashing blue lights. I could hear them whispering. Something about lemons.

Megaphone screeched. "Sir, you've been in there a while. How many hostages do you have?"

Checked my pockets. Both sausages, still secure.

"Two! Back off! My family will be freed! You can't keep them forever you sour bastards!"

Tossed a grenade out the door, carefully taking cover behind it.

"Sir, no need to throw fruit at us! Are you hungry? Can we get you a pizza?"

Pizza? Now? Yes! Backup!

"Pizza Palace! The kind one! A pony, with lemons!"

There was a brief pause.

"Sir, I don't understand? What pony?"

"Lemons! Pony pineapple lawnmower! Two thousand chicken burgers!"

"Sir, calm down. How about you trade us one hostage, and we will get you a cheese pizza? Deal? But that's far too many chicken burgers! We just can't do it!"

"Deal. I'm sending out the sausage now. I want two thousand lemons, a lemoncopter with citric fuel and a private island for me and Frank."

Tossed a sausage from my pocket outside. Nobody moved to collect him. Just left him to lie there, on the floor, cold and alone.

Cold, alone, sour. Bitter. Australia.

Screeching megaphone blasted out my ringing ears once more. "Sir... That's a sausage?"

Suddenly, tactical lemon warriors armed with shotguns burst in through the back door, then the front. I dived for cover behind the desk, heart pounding in my eyes.

"Down! Get down! Drop the weapon!"

"No! Never! Release my family! Open the vault! The lemons! THE LEMONS!"

Rose up from cover, gun trained on a lemon warrior. No use—misfire. No blasters, no lasers.

Sound from his shotgun rang out through the entire bank, cacophony sour in my ears and eyes. Blast hit me in the chest, bitter agony, sour darkness.

Chapter 22

Fog. Haze. Daze.

Eyes open. Janet?

"There you are, sleepyhead. About time."

"Janet? Where was... What are... What's—"

"All these questions Marty. You know I hate you, right?"

"Wait... What?"

"Yeah, I know. Sorry Marty, but I do. The way Hannah looks at you? I asked you to take another job and you wouldn't do it. I'm supposed to be your wife, but I have to sit here and think about her fucking you with her eyes. You're a sour cunt, Marty."

"No... I... I would never, I didn't, I couldn't—"

"All you had to do was leave that bank. Go drive a lorry, or something, I don't know. All of this? You chose it. You're responsible."

"No... No I'm not—I didn't—"

"Doesn't matter. I'm still gone. I got the money, I got Jessica, and you? All you have is lemons. Now wake up, busy day ahead of you."

Bitter tang of pain rang through my head and chest. Couldn't move my arm, metal cuffs clipped me to the bed I found myself in.

Bright, white lights glaring at me from the ceiling, the walls. Sour stench of disinfectant zesting my nose.

Looked down. Blue gown, bare feet, chairs. Curtain, blue, not a single lemon in sight.

Silence felt weirdly oppressive. Stared at the white wall as it stared right back. Really wish I could talk to Frank right now. Just wanted someone to listen.

Dark outside. Time lost all meaning. Had it been hours or days? Or more?

Door opened, nurse walked in. Lemon blonde hair, piercing green emerald eyes. Could hear beeping from various machines out in the hallway.

She jolted. "Oh! You're awake!"

"No, I'm Martin."

"How are you feeling?"

"With my hands, usually."

Narrowed her gaze. "Right... Do you know where you are? What happened?"

"I do. Gary and the lemon legionnaires escaped from Frank and assaulted me. It was kind of a blur, but Gary gave me a journal. It implicated Hannah... Wait..."

Did it, though? Did it really?

No. Janet blamed Hannah. But the lemons didn't. The lemons blamed Janet. Is that what Gary had been trying to get through my thick skull all this time?

Fuck.

Nurse disappeared. Fetched some kind of man, wearing some kind of clothing.

"Martin Fletcher? DCI Roberts. You gave us all a scare there. Either the biggest practical joke since Brexit or you need some serious therapy mate."

"Didn't vote on that. Didn't understand it. Seemed a bit of a sour subject."

"How are you feeling, then? Bet your chest is sore. Head too, I'll expect. You took a baton round square between the ribs mate. Must smart something fierce."

"Yeah. Tangs. I don't eat batons, though, more of a baguette guy."

"Right. So anyway, spoke to the toxicologist. You like to party, Marty?"

Ha! Punny. Curled up a grin.

"Used to. Took my daughter to the playground all the time. Until she... She's gone now. Australia."

Chest hurt even more.

"I see. Fan of mushrooms?"

"Only in risotto. Never been to a concert. Sometimes have them on pizza. Bought some from a celebrity chef recently. Tasted chewy."

Scratching from his pen on his notebook like chalk on a chalkboard. Or nails? Nail? Mail?

"Mr Fletcher? Please, answer the question."

"I'm sorry. I didn't see it. Can you ask me the answer again?"

More scratching. Tired. So tired.

Oh fuck. The lemon legion. The war. What... What happened?

"Did you stop him? Did you get Gary? Is Frank OK?"

The detective sat next to me, asking me various questions. I explained it all as he wrote, every bitter word, every sour situation.

"We read the journal, Martin. Last we found, your wife was in Mexico. We were investigating you initially, until the truth became clear. You have Juliet to thank for that."

"The truth? Did you finally catch Hannah? Did the lemons finally pay? I have to thank Janet for what exactly?"

"Your wife, Mr Fletcher? Criminal, fraudster, a connected one. She stole absolutely thousands. Sorry."

"Lemons. Lemons. LEMONS! LEMONS LEMONS LEMONS—"

Nurse gave me a...something. Sleepy now. Just close my eyes, just for a quick zest.

Chapter 23

Time passed, increments, standard units. How much of it I couldn't say.

Stared at the walls of my new... Home? Whatever this place was. It wasn't a prison, but it may as well have been. Lonely without Frank's cheerful humming.

Not a lemon in sight. No bitter tang in my nose, no sour citrus clutching at my throat or clawing at my eyes.

Nothing but the bitter tang of truth.

Lesbian. Husband. Jessica. Australia. Or was it Mexico? Or Morocco? Or the Maldives?

Christ fucking knows. Think Frank probably has more of an idea than I do, and he's just a bloody fridge. Miss him, really do.

"Good morning, Martin," the kind nurse lady said, barging into my room. "How are we today, dear?"

"Alive. Wish I wasn't."

"Aww. Still feeling sour?"

"Not funny, Janet."

Cruel twist of fate she had the same name as my evil bitch cunt fraudster wife. About wretched every time the word left my bastard mouth.

"Well, it's been nearly a month you've been with us now. Feeling any better?"

Good bloody question, to be honest. Dosed me up on some shite, seemed to... Calm. A little, at least. Guess I didn't really know.

"Much," I said, meaning it. Maybe. Probably not.

"Aww. Well, I'm sure we'll have you feeling zesty again in no time, lemon man!"

"Piss off, Janet."

Giggled as she buggered off, for the umpteenth time. Fuck knows how long I'd been here. Could be a long time.

She might have said, actually. Not that I was listening. Still too many things buzzing around in my head, bitter thoughts fighting for the front seat.

Couldn't sleep. Without Frank's gentle humming I just couldn't settle. Hadn't seen William in a long time either. Or Janet. Hope she's OK.

Wait, no I don't. Fuck you, Janet. Give me my fucking daughter and my savings back, and take a nice relaxing bath in a volcano.

Lemons lurked. Not here, not in this room, but somewhere. Close my eyes and I can smell them. Fragments of fever dreams lingered on my lips as I spoke the name.

"Gary."

Need to get out of here. Soon, if I can. Haven't sat alone with my thoughts since I was born, and don't want to start now.

Part of me wished I could hop on a bus and go see that chef again. Chef or drug dealer, if you'll believe the inspector chap who lectured me hours on end. Heard about six words of it.

Days I wondered what was real. But that police lemon man promised to come and see me, so I waited. Thought about scratching the days on the wall, but I'd been here too many to count already. Think it might have been twelve.

"Frank, mate. Hope you're staying strong out there. I miss you."

He couldn't hear me, but that didn't stop him listening. Needed to get out of here. Soon.

Closed my eyes, laughing lemons lying beneath them. Point and laugh all you want, bitter little buggers. Need the sleep.

Days continued passing me by in the blink of an eye. Or weeks? Couldn't tell. Time lost all meaning without the gentle hum of Frank or irritating yet endearing advice of William sour music to my ears.

"Janette, can I use the phone now? I miss William and Frank."

I was wearing her down. She'd let me call her Janette for starters, just to try and separate her from my fraudster bitch wife.

"Well, you've been responding well to treatment. Dr Butcher said you can use the landline, but only with my supervision."

Had to chuckle at the name. Bet the smarmy git only went to medical school to be a doctor butcher. Still, couldn't judge, I might have done the same. Maybe I should have been Mr Fletcher the blacksmith? That could—

"Martin?"

"Sorry, off with the lemons. What did you say?"

"Landline?"

"Oh. That won't work."

Raised her eyebrow. "What do you mean?"

"Don't know William's number."

Narrowed her gaze. "Then... How do you call him?"

"I... I... Open the phone, and he's... There..."

Oh. Fuck.

Not fucking real, is he? No, worse than that. Open the phone, talk to him in the fucking windows and mirrors and he's my FUCKING REFLECTION! FUCK!

"LEMONS! FUCKING LEMONS! LEMONS LEMONS LEMONS—"

Sharp ting of pain as the needle stabbed me. Sleepy.

Chapter 24

"You've got a visitor, Marty," Janette said as she came inside, Roberts in tow.

Looked a lot better without his tactical lemon battle gear on. Or I might have imagined that, I really don't remember.

"Hey Martin. Good to see you. You're looking a bit less, well, bonkers."

Couldn't help but chuckle. Had a directness about him that filled me full of zest.

"Feeling it. I think, anyway."

"Well you're not currently waving a banana around a bank or chucking lemons at people, so it's a vast improvement."

Chuckled again. Man should be a therapist. Or a comedian. Or a comediapist? Therapian? No idea. I miss my daughter.

"So I'm afraid that's just, well. I don't really know how else to put it."

Bugger. Missed that.

"Missed what, mate? Off with the lemons."

"Figured. You do this thing with your chin when you're not paying attention. Kinda cute actually. Right, well, we're officially giving up finding your wife and daughter."

Wait. What?

"But... But why? But she's a villain, she's a—"

"Mate, I'm the choir, and you're preaching to me. She belongs in here far more than you do. But we simply can't keep up with her, and for all we know she could be anywhere by now. I'm sorry, Marty."

Lemons clutched at my throat. Gasping for air. Eyes, streamed bitter citric acid.

More time passed. Roberts was gone. Janette was back.

"Feeling any better today, Marty?"

"What? Where's—where's Roberts?"

"That was yesterday, silly. Swear your memory's getting better."

"Don't you mean worse?"

"Yes? I said that. You OK Marty?"

No.

"Yes."

"Good, because you have another visitor."

Oh god. Oh no.

Rushed to my feet. "Hannah, I'm so sorry I—"

Didn't say anything. Just rushed over. Hugged me close, tight, warm. For a fleeting, bitter moment my broken pieces were back together.

"I've been so worried about you, Marty. I missed you. Even if you did hold up my bank with a banana."

"Right. Uh, sorry about that. Was going—I am going—through a lot."

"No shit."

She started giggling. Couldn't help it, joined in with her. Infectious, really.

"So... Marty, I found myself thinking about things. Lots of things. Wasn't fair how I just, enjoyed my time with you, and pushed you away at the bank. I want you. Want us. I have for the longest time."

Lemon printed journal. Confession. Obsession.

Looked into her eyes. Blue as the ocean, twinkle of the stars. Her lips, red as cherry. Skin, pale as moonlight. Her hair, blonde as lemon.

Lemons.

Bitter stench of citrus in my nose. Taste of acid in my throat. Swallowed hard. Looked her in the eye.

"Yeah. Me too. If I ever get out of here."

Held my hand, gently kissed my cheek. "You will. Talked to Dr Butcher already. You keep trying, you'll be out of here in a month. I've already marked the discharge date on my calendar, and you're taking me to dinner. But Marty?"

"Yes, dear?"

"No fucking lemons, yeah?"

Curled up a grin. Chuckle in my throat cleared the bitter citric tang. Smile in my eyes.

Time soon passed. First night in a long while, sleep came easy. Well, easier, anyway. Still miss you, Frank. William too.

Chapter 25

Blinked twice, next month passed me by in a sour haze.

"Dr Butcher signed your discharge forms, Martin. Don't get sour out there, and call us if you need anything. Bye bye lemon man."

"Piss off, Janette. Maybe go get laid, stop you being such a bitter cow."

She laughed out loud. "Oh, that an invitation?"

Shook my head. "Nope. Date of my own. Later."

Headed off, before long, key in the door.

"Frank, mate. Good to hear you humming again. I missed you, buddy."

Didn't respond. Couldn't—just a fridge.

Looked at myself in the mirror.

"If you're in there, William, cheers for everything. You were... Something, I guess. Not that I ever listened, hey."

No reply. Felt like talking to myself. Left me a little hollow, a little bitter.

Call came in. Hannah.

"Marty, you got home OK?"

"Yeah. See you tonight? Half eight?"

"Absolutely. Red dress dry cleaned, just for you. See you soon, handsome. Might even have a banana for me later?"

"If I'm lucky."

Clicked the call away. Somehow left me feeling a little sour.

Hopped in my car, headed off. Wallet in my pocket, clothes on my back. Picture of Jessica beside me.

Drive there was tense. Gripped my wheel tight, flash of Hannah in her red dress. Beautiful.

Finally arrived and took out my bottle of pills. Tossed them in the river.

Phone out. Vision of Hannah, beautiful in a wedding dress, eyes deep as the ocean flashed in my mind. Eyes as deep as the ocean. Love as strong as the trunk of a lemon tree. Beautiful, blonde hair. Lemon blonde hair. Lemons.

Tossed my phone in the river. Landed with a bitter plop.

Boarded the plane. No luggage. No plan. No idea. But I would find her. The lemons willed it, and lemons?

Lemons tell no lies.

Printed in Dunstable, United Kingdom